Farrah nodded. "All right. Thanks."

He cupped her chin in his hand before leaning down and capturing her mouth in a kiss that she felt all the way to her toes. His tongue tangled with hers, eliciting all kinds of lust that began rushing through her veins in a matter of seconds.

When he finally released her mouth and stepped back, she eased back down to the edge of the bed to watch him get dressed. He slid his jeans back over his muscular thighs before readjusting his briefs. She studied the bulge in his crotch, the object that had given her so much pleasure over the past year. It was still hard, thick and so engorged it practically seemed ready to explode.

Desire thrummed through her body as she remembered how good he felt inside of her, how good he tasted, and she quickly decided there was no use letting a good opportunity go to waste

"Xavier?"

He glanced over at ...
"Yes?"

"How about one mo...

*Beyond Temptation
*Risky Pleasures
In Bed with the Boss
*Irresistible Forces
Just Deserts
The Object of His Protection
Temperatures Rising
*Intimate Seduction
Bachelor Untamed
*Hidden Pleasures
Star of His Heart
Bachelor Unleashed

*Steele Family titles

BRENDA JACKSON

is a die "heart" romantic who married her childhood sweetheart and still proudly wears the "going steady" ring he gave her when she was fifteen. Because she's always believed in the power of love, Brenda's stories always have happy endings. In her real-life love story, Brenda and Gerald, her husband of thirty-eight years, live in Jacksonville, Florida, and have two sons.

A *New York Times* bestselling author of more than seventy-five romance titles, Brenda is a retiree from a major insurance company and now divides her time between family, writing and traveling with Gerald. You may write to Brenda at P.O. Box 28267, Jacksonville, Florida 32226 or her email address, WriterBJackson@aol.com, or visit her website at www.brendajackson.net.

BRENDA JACKSON

"

Bachelor Unleashed

KIMANI
ROMANCE™

To the love of my life, Gerald Jackson, Sr.

 KIMANI PRESS™

Recycling programs
for this product may
not exist in your area.

ISBN-13: 978-0-373-86188-0

BACHELOR UNLEASHED

www.kimanipress.com

Printed in U.S.A.

Dear Reader,

When I first introduced Xavier Kane in *Risky Pleasures* (Vanessa Steele and Cameron Cody's love story), I was already imagining the kind of love interest he would have. Then, while writing *Intimate Seduction* (Donovan's story) and introducing Farrah (Natalie's best friend), I knew I had found the woman for Xavier.

Bachelor Unleashed is Xavier and Farrah's story. It's a love affair started in *Intimate Seduction,* where hints were given as to where things were headed in *Bachelor Untamed.* Both have reasons for not wanting to become involved in a serious relationship, but when it comes to true love, this couple finds out that they can only follow their hearts.

And don't worry if you haven't read any of the previous books—this is a wonderful stand-alone story, as well.

I hope you enjoy reading Xavier and Farrah's story as much as I enjoyed writing it.

Happy reading!

Brenda Jackson

ACKNOWLEDGMENTS

Special thanks to Sharon Beaner, who took the time to enlighten me about the job of a mediator. This one is especially for you.

Give, and it will be given to you. A good measure, pressed down, shaken together and running over, will be poured into your lap.
—*Luke* 6:38

Prologue

There was nothing a woman was left wanting before, during and after making love with Xavier Kane. And Farrah Langley was caught now in the throes of one of those heated, satisfying moments.

She had known she was in for a sensual treat the minute she'd opened the door to him earlier. With a bottle of wine in his hand, he'd stood there looking sexier than any man had a right to look, arriving for what had become known as one of his infamous booty calls. Now with three orgasms behind her in less than an hour and her body climbing greedily toward a fourth, she reached the conclusion that Xavier Kane was a pleasure-producing maniac.

They were in the middle of her bed, on top of the covers, naked, soaked in perspiration, their limbs entwined, their bodies connected, making out like sex-deprived addicts who couldn't get enough of each other. It was always this endless need that drove them out of control and over the edge. Something about the feel of his hot, sweaty flesh rubbing against hers as he thrust in and out of her body made her g-spot literally weep.

The room exuded the scent of raw sex, the aroma of a virile man, and she was drenched in the fragrance of a deeply satisfied woman. A woman who was his most willing partner and was doing everything to keep up with him. The man's sexual appetite was voracious, and he delivered just as much as he procured. She had no complaints, just compliments. Xavier definitely knew how to conduct business in the bedroom.

It was storming outside, and they were having their own monsoon inside. Only with him did she experience such a downpour of torrential sensations, such a deluge of emotions…some she knew were best kept under wraps. But he had a way of pulling them out of her anyway. He had the ability to make her want things she was better off not having. More than once with him she'd let her guard down, allowed her body's own greedy wants and needs to betray her, which was a transgression that could cost her.

It was nearly two years since her divorce from Dustin Holloway had become final. Dustin, her college sweetheart, a man she had vowed to always love. A man who'd vowed to love her forever as well. But four years into their marriage she'd begun noticing things. Like him wearing a scent that wasn't hers. Him moaning out a strange name during sex, and him sneaking out of bed in the wee hours of the night to make private calls on his cell phone.

She had finally confronted him, and without any remorse, he'd confessed that for the past two years he'd been living a double life. He not only had a mistress but also a child, and he wanted a divorce to marry the other woman and be a father to his daughter.

It had taken a full year for the hurt to go away, and she would admit remnants of it still lingered, making her cautious, wary and adamant even at twenty-seven years of age never to give her heart to another man again.

"Let your pleasure rip for me now, Farrah."

Xavier's deep, husky command struck a delicious chord, sent sensuous shivers up her spine, sank deep into her sensitive flesh and touched her everywhere, especially at the juncture of her thighs where their bodies were joined.

She forgot everything except how he was making her feel. Her body fragmented into a cascade of gratifying prisms that ran from the top of her head to the soles of her feet. She was flooded with more sensations than she could sink her teeth into…so she sank them into him, biting his shoulder as she found herself drowning in total and complete sensual abandonment.

It was then that he skillfully lifted her hips in order to thrust deeper into a spot he always reserved for last. Her legs tightened around his waist, and she released one hellacious scream as pleasure tore through her.

Farrah was convinced his ear drums were damage-proof, just as she figured the power and strength of his erection should be patented. While she let go and continued to take one merciless fall into ecstatic oblivion, she knew the moment the sexual tension that had been building inside him popped, and with it went his control. His body responded to hers, and following her lead, he went off the deep end. His thrusts became harder, stronger, went deeper, and his hold on her tightened as she locked him between her thighs. And then came the Xavier Kane growl that pierced the air and only made her want him even more.

"Xavier, please. More."

And he continued to give her more, giving in to her shameless plea. Heat built as he stroked her while pushing her thighs apart with his knee to go even deeper. His thrusts were the strokes of rapture, and the skill with which he was delivering them was the pinnacle of pure sensual delight. They were what continued to spark that foolishness in her head that whispered what they were sharing was more than just great sex. It was about a man and woman so in tune to each other's wants and needs, so in harmony to each other's desires that practically anything—a touch, a lick, a breathless groan—nipped at their nerve endings and pushed them to this.

As she continued to tumble over the edge, she didn't want to be reminded that he'd become her weakness, nor that she'd made a decision as to how she would handle it. As much as she preferred not taking such drastic actions, her decision was one that couldn't be helped. Not if she wanted to retain her sanity and peace of mind. And she couldn't put it off any longer.

Tonight she would end things between them.

She pushed the thought to the back of her mind. She didn't want to dwell on all the pleasurable lovemaking hours she would be giving up. She would just have to learn to deal with it.

For now she wanted nothing more than to keep falling into the most sensuous waters a woman's body could plunge.

Xavier reluctantly eased out of Farrah's body, sighed deeply and then slid out of bed. The first thing he noticed was that it was no longer storming outside. Calm had settled over the earth.

The second thing he noticed was the absence of Farrah's even breathing, which meant even after all those powerful orgasms she was still awake. Usually she would have fallen into an exhausted sleep.

He glanced over his shoulder and met her hazy gaze and thought he saw two things in the dark depths of her eyes—regret and resolve.

"We need to talk, Xavier," she said softly.

For some reason he didn't like the sound of that. Usually when a woman informed a man they needed to talk right after they'd made love it meant she had a bomb to drop. The first crazy notion that ran through his mind was that she was going to tell him that somehow, although she was on the pill and he always wore a condom, she'd gotten pregnant. The chances of that happening were probably less than one percent, but it was the one percent that had him feeling kind of nervous right now.

He studied her features and thought, as he always had, that she was an utterly beautiful woman who wore that "just made love to" look well. And just the thought that he'd given her that look, dressed her in it real good, sent primitive shivers of male pride and possessiveness down his spine. Hell, if he was a cave man, he would be beating on his damn chest about now.

"Let me take care of things in the bathroom first and then I'll be right back," he said. And with every step toward the bathroom he couldn't help wondering what this discussion would be about.

If she was going to inform him that he was going to be a daddy, the thought didn't send him into panic for some reason. He was thirty-two, closer to thirty-three if you wanted to be more specific, and he was pretty well-off, so he could handle child support payments without breaking a sweat, just as long as a woman didn't try taking him to the cleaners. He knew, after being Farrah's lover for almost a year, that she was not the greedy type.

Except for when they were in bed. Between the sheets, her sexual appetite could just about rival his. But he had no complaints. And he knew that, like him, she had this thing about commitments. They'd both gotten burned once, he with an ex-girlfriend and she an ex-husband, so a no-strings affair was all they'd ever wanted from each other.

They hadn't meant for things to last as long as they had. He'd been with her longer than any other woman… except Dionne Witherspoon. However, he refused to go there tonight. He would not think about the woman he'd fallen in love with while attending law school at Harvard. Dionne had only sought out his affections so he could provide the help she needed for her law exams. Once she aced them all, she had dropped him like a hot potato.

Xavier returned from the bathroom a short while later accepting there was a strong possibility that, regardless of whether he and Farrah wanted to play the commitment game or not, they would be forced to do so if she was pregnant. After all, he much preferred being a real father to his child rather than just a child support check. He wanted to be the type of parent to his child that his father had been to him. Benjamin Kane had been a top-notch dad. He still was.

Instead of getting back in bed, Xavier picked up his jeans and slid into them, then he eased down in the wingback chair across the room from the bed. He had followed Farrah's lead. She was no longer naked but was wearing a robe. It was short and showed a lot of thigh. He thought she had luscious thighs, the kind a man loved to hold on to and ride. Farrah Langley made any man with red hot testosterone appreciate being a man. Hell, he was getting another hard-on just looking at her.

"Tonight was it for us, Xavier."

He pulled his gaze from her thighs to her face, not sure he had heard her correctly. He stared at her for a long, silent moment, and when he saw the regret and resolve he'd caught a glimpse of earlier, he asked, "What did you say?"

She sat down on the side of her bed to face him. "I said, tonight was it."

He fought to keep back the shock from his face. "It?"

"Yes. We started this thing between us almost a year ago, longer than either of us intended. It was never meant to last more than a couple of months, if even that."

He nodded, knowing that much was true. For him the practice of self-preservation was a way of life. He abhorred emotional involvements of any kind. He and Farrah had established the boundaries up front, basically on that first night.

And he could recall that first night well...

They had met at the Racetrack Café, a popular hangout here in Charlotte. He'd been there with a close friend by the name of Donovan Steele, and Farrah had been with her best friend, Natalie Ford. Before the night was over, Donovan and Natalie had paired off and so had he and Farrah. He'd thought she was ultrabeautiful, hot. There had been something about her that had immediately made his mouth water, his tongue tingle, and he'd known from the jump that he wanted some of her. And he had been able to tell from her body language that the feeling was mutual.

A few nights later he had shown up at her front door with a bottle of wine in his hand and a hard-on in his pants. She had opened the door and let him in, fully aware of the nature of his visit. And things had been that way between them since. No commitment, just great sex.

And now she wanted to end things.

Before he could fix his mouth to ask why, she said in a teasing voice that he really didn't find amusing, "I wouldn't want to threaten your standing as a member of that club."

He knew exactly what club she was referring to. It was one he and his five godbrothers had formed a few years ago—the Bachelors in Demand Club. They were men who enjoyed their single lives with no plans of settling down. All six of them had their own issues with commitment and were basically guarding their hearts. Now there were only five of them left, since one of his godbrothers, Uriel Lassiter, had gotten married last year.

"Donovan and Natalie's wedding reminded me of all the reasons why I don't want to be seriously involved with anyone again," she went on to add.

He drew in a deep breath. As much as he preferred things continuing between them for a little while longer, the decision to split now was hers to make, and he respected that. And then maybe she was right. Things had lasted longer than either of them had planned, and things were beginning to get too complacent between them. Hell, he could recall speeding away from Uriel's wedding reception like a mad man trying to make it to her place. And wasn't it just last weekend they had literally burned the sheets off the bed at the Ritz-Carlton in New York after Donovan and Natalie's wedding reception?

He didn't need a rocket scientist to see that things could start getting serious between them if they weren't careful. She had the ability to unleash feelings within him he preferred staying locked away. So maybe they should make a clean break before things got messy and complicated. Those were two words he didn't like having in his vocabulary.

He eased out of the chair and stood. "Hey, no problem. It was nice while it lasted, sweetheart." He not only meant that from the bottom of his heart, but also from the head of his penis that was already swelling in protest with his words. He was definitely going to miss sharing all those bedroom hours with her.

"You do understand, right?"

"Of course I do," he said, ignoring the tightening in his chest. He slowly crossed the room and reached out and pulled her into his arms. "I will always appreciate our time together and if you ever need me for anything, you know how to reach me. Don't ever hesitate to call, all right?"

Farrah nodded. "All right. Thanks."

He cupped her chin in his hand before leaning down and capturing her mouth in a kiss that she felt all the way to her toes. She thought being a good kisser was just another quality he possessed. His tongue tangling with hers elicited all kinds of lust that began rushing through her veins in a matter of seconds. It didn't take much to get her wet again.

When he finally released her mouth to step back, she eased back down on the edge of the bed to watch him dress. He slid his jeans back down his tight, muscular thighs before grabbing his briefs to put them on. Her gaze studied his erection, the object that had given her so much pleasure over the past year. It was still hard, thick and so engorged its veins seemed ready to explode.

Desire thrummed through her, and she began remembering how his shaft felt inside of her, how good it tasted, and she quickly decided there was no use letting a good hard-on go to waste. Especially since it was one she wouldn't be seeing again. "Xavier?"

He glanced over at her as he reached for his jeans. "Yes?"

"How about one more for the road?"

A slow smiled tugged at the corners of what she thought was a pair of ultrasexy lips. She watch him slide underwear back down his legs and toss them aside before walking back over to her. He then said in a deep, husky voice, "Baby, I'll give you something better than one more for the road. Get ready because we're about to take flight. I'm about to take you on the ride of your life on the interstate."

And with that said, he tumbled her back onto the rumpled bedcovers.

Chapter 1

Six months later

"So, what are your plans for the holidays, X?"

Xavier leaned back in the leather chair and propped his legs up on his desk while glancing out the window at New York City's skyline. The Empire State Building was in his direct line of vision and looked massive against the dark blue sky overhead.

He had arrived in New York a few days ago to wrap up a business deal between the Northeast Division of Cody Enterprises and Oxley Financial Services. Cameron Cody's takeover of the investment firm was a done deal, and as the executive attorney for all Cameron's affairs, Xavier needed to be in place to make sure everything was handled as it should be. Not only was he considered

Cameron's right-hand man, they were very close friends. That friendship had begun back at Harvard when the two had been struggling students, determined to become successful in life.

And now, just like then, they looked out for each other, so he wasn't surprised by Cameron's question. Cameron knew that Xavier's parents had left for their annual six-month missionary crusade—this year to Haiti—and wouldn't be returning back to the States until sometime in the spring. "I'm not sure yet, Cam. I have a number of invitations out there."

Cameron's deep chuckle sounded over the speaker-phone. "Hey, don't brag about it. Not everyone is blessed to have five sets of godparents."

A frown settled on Xavier's face that was best not seen by anyone. "That could be a blessing or a curse," he said, shaking his head pensively. "Currently it might be the latter. Now that Uriel has married, some of the godparents are eyeing the remaining five of us. I'm not sure I want to be included in any of their get-togethers for the holidays. Thanksgiving was hard enough."

"I bet."

Everyone had been invited to Uriel and Ellie's place on Cavanaugh Lake. Former neighbors on the lake, the two had remodeled both their homes once married, combining them into one with an enclosed walkway. That meant plenty of space for sleepovers.

And it was nice having all six godfathers present as they retold the story of how they'd met at Morehouse and become close friends, and how on graduation day they'd promised to stay in touch by becoming godfathers to each of their children, and that the firstborn sons' names would carry the letters of the alphabet from U to Z. And that was how Uriel Lassiter, Virgil Bougard, Winston Coltrane, Xavier Kane, York Ellis and Zion Blackstone had come into existence.

"Well, you know you can add me and Vanessa to your list," Cam was saying. "You're always welcome to our place. We're doing Christmas in Jamaica this year."

Xavier couldn't help but smile. His friend sounded happy and contented. What man wouldn't be once he'd finally gotten the woman of his dreams? The former Vanessa Steele had been determined not to become involved with Cameron after his attempt to take over her family's business. Cameron, on the other hand, had been just as determined to win her over. Not surprisingly, Cam had succeeded and was a happily married man with a baby on the way.

"Thanks, Cam, but I think I'm going to use the two weeks I'll have off during the holidays to chill and relax. I'm even thinking about going someplace quiet. I might decide to visit Zion in Rome," he said.

Moments later after hanging up the phone with Cameron, Xavier stood to stretch, ignoring the pile of work sitting on his desk. Not only was he executive attorney to Cameron Cody, he also managed the legal affairs for several well-known Hollywood celebrities, which was the reason he had an office in Los Angeles as well.

Of all his clients, Cam kept him the busiest, which

accounted for Xavier's additional offices in London, Jamaica and Paris. And since Cameron's newest brother-in-law, Quade Westmoreland, had a first cousin who was married to a sheikh, Cameron and Sheikh Jamal Yasir were anticipating a business venture that could now take Xavier to parts of the Middle East.

"Mr. Kane, those reports you ordered are ready."

He glanced over at the intercom on his desk before leaning over to press a button. "Thanks, Vicki. Please bring them in."

"With pleasure, sir."

Xavier shook his head. Vicki Connell, the woman who'd replaced Christine James, his New York administrative assistant, while she was out on an extended maternity leave, was determined to get inside his pants one way or the other. He knew the signs and had read those hidden seductive looks in her pretty dark eyes plenty of times whenever he came to town. All of that would be fine and dandy if he was interested, but he wasn't. And he downright hated admitting that he hadn't been gung ho about any woman getting into his pants since splitting with Farrah almost a half a year ago.

He didn't know what the hell was wrong with him since, typically, he wasn't the brooding type. He'd certainly never given a woman any lasting thoughts once things between them had ended. So why was he doing so now?

He walked over to the window and glanced out again. If the forecaster's predictions held true, a snowstorm would be hitting the city by Sunday, and Xavier wished he could return to Charlotte before that happened. He could kiss that wish goodbye since he was due to remain in New York for another week or so.

He heard the door opening behind him and then an ultra sexy feminine voice said, "Here are the reports, Mr. Kane. Will there be anything else?"

He slowly turned around at the same time Vicki was smoothing her short skirt down her thighs, at least as much of them that could be covered. He was convinced if she were to bend over he would find out what color her panties were.

He had to admit her outfit looked fine on her, but did nothing for him, other than reminding him how inappropriate it was for the workplace. But then the same thing held true for the outfit she'd worn yesterday. One of his godbrothers, York, who lived in New York, had dropped by the office to take him to lunch and had mentioned a number of times during their meal how good he thought Vicki had looked. Apparently he was impressed with her attire.

"Yes, there will be something else," Xavier replied to Vicki. As he spoke he watched lust flare in her eyes.

"Yes?" she asked, with anticipation flowing in her voice.

"Please have a seat."

She lifted a brow. "A seat?"

"Yes."

"In the chair?"

He inwardly smiled. Evidently she'd been hoping he

meant spread-eagle on the desk. "Yes, Vicki, please sit in the chair."

When she did so, the hem of her skirt barely covered her thighs. "Yes, Mr. Kane?"

"How old are you, Vicki?"

After probably trying to figure out why he was asking, she said, "I'm twenty."

He nodded as he leaned against his desk. "And I understand you're attending classes at the university at night and working for a temp agency part-time."

She shifted in her seat to deliberately show more of a bare thigh. "Yes, that's right. I'm hoping to get hired here full-time during the summer so I can qualify for an internship next fall."

He wasn't surprised to hear that. Cody Enterprises had several internship programs available. Going to college had been a financial hardship for Cameron, so he was a firm believer in assisting college students whatever way he could. The internship program he had in place was just one way of doing so.

"I see no reason why that can't happen for you, other than for one."

She looked surprised. "And what reason is that?"

"You need to improve your attire in the work-place."

She actually looked offended. "I was told there wasn't a dress code here."

"There isn't one per se. However, a person trying to move up in a company needs to care about the image she projects."

She lifted her chin. "And just what kind of image am I projecting?"

"An image of someone who enjoys getting a lot of attention. You've become a distraction. Deliberately so. Every man in this building finds some excuse to come to this floor every day and your work is suffering because you're spending more time entertaining than taking care of business matters. I've yet to get that report that was due yesterday."

"It's not my fault those guys drop by and take up my time."

Xavier's gaze roamed up and down her outfit. "Isn't it?"

He didn't say anything, wanting to give her time to consider everything he'd said. "That will be all for now, Vicki," he finally said. "I hope we don't have to discuss this issue again and I hope to have that report on my desk before I leave today."

He took his seat behind his desk and watched her quickly leave the room. Moments later, while sitting staring into space, the truth hit him right between the eyes as to why he wasn't attracted to other women. He hadn't gotten Farrah out of his system.

Considering everything they'd shared for close to a year, that was understandable. Usually his affairs with women rarely lasted a couple of months. That was when the women began to get possessive, and Xavier had no interest in being tied down to one woman.

With Farrah things had been quite different. She'd never stamped a claim to any kind of ownership on him. He'd liked that. He'd liked her. And dammit, he missed her. He still wasn't sure why she had ended things between them, but he did have a hunch.

They had started getting too comfortable with each other, had fallen into one of those relationship routines where they just couldn't get enough of each other. That sort of addiction between two people was kind of scary since there was no telling where it could lead. Straight to their hearts was out of the question since falling in love was in neither of their plans. Still, the thought of doing something as drastic as ending things between them hadn't crossed his mind.

He'd been perfectly satisfied with how things had been going. She didn't ask for anything but gave everything. Hell, no woman could compare to her in the bedroom. And she had never questioned his activities when they weren't together. But then in his mind she'd had exclusive rights as his bed partner, although he'd never given them to her verbally. It had been something understood between them. He'd known she hadn't dated anyone else during the time he'd been her lover, and neither had he.

He reached for the report Vicki had delivered to him and, after flipping through a few pages, decided his concentration level wasn't where it needed to be today. This was New York. There was no reason he couldn't get back in the groove and begin enjoying life again. He had the phone number of a few ladies living here who were laid back and easy. The latter was the key word. He should give one a call, invite her to meet him somewhere for a drink. And then afterward, they could go to her place for a roll between the sheets. Hell, skip the drink, he would just go for the roll between the sheets. He hadn't had sex with a woman since Farrah. What was he waiting on? Christmas?

He glanced over at his calendar. And speaking of Christmas…it was only three weeks away, so if he was waiting on Christmas, he didn't have long, but he doubted his testosterone could last until then.

Xavier shrugged off the feeling that something was missing in his life. Instead, he thought about the woman he would pay a visit later tonight. Beth Logan was a flight attendant he'd met a couple of years ago and was a sure bet if she was in town. It wouldn't bother her in the least that they hadn't connected in over a year. She was known to be hot and ready whenever they got together in one of their uninhibited passionate romps.

He smiled. Yes, making a booty call tonight was definitely in order. All he needed was to stop somewhere to grab a bottle of wine, and he would be all set.

"So there you have it, Farrah," Frank McGraw said, handing the file to her. "The judge recommended the women seek mediation before officially going to court."

Farrah nodded as she scanned the file. She'd reviewed it already while on the plane from Charlotte since Frank's secretary had faxed a copy to her that morning before her flight. The case was interesting. Two best friends from high school, Kerrie Shaw and Lori Byers, had started a line of cosmetics right after college, investing equally in the start-up. Lori had eventually lost interest when she married and became a mother. Kerrie, still single, had continued to make the business prosper and, with Lori's blessings, had even moved things in another direction when she created an antiaging cream. Though Lori hadn't been actively involved in the company in over ten years, her new husband wanted Kerrie to buy out Lori's share at a percentage Kerrie felt was unreasonable, considering she was the one who'd made CL cosmetics into the mega-company it was today.

"So what do you think?" Frank broke into Farrah's concentration to ask.

She glanced up. "Like all the others, I find this case interesting."

"Well, you're the best damn mediator this firm has. I'm just glad you were able to change your schedule to accommodate us."

Farrah smiled. "What woman would turn down a chance to come to New York, especially in December? I plan to do some major holiday shopping while I'm here."

Frank chuckled. "Good luck. Forecasters predict a snowstorm by Sunday. Personally, I think it might be before then. If that happens, you won't get much shopping done."

Farrah stood, stuffing the file into her messenger case. "Hey, no problem. If that happens, then I'll stay in my hotel room with a bottle of wine and a good mystery novel and be just as happy. Then I'll fly out as planned and return next week to wrap up things when the weather is more cooperative. When I return I'll just tack on a few additional days for shopping and a Broadway show."

Frank smiled. "That sounds nice." He leaned back in his chair. The look in his eyes shifted from professional to predatory. "How about dinner tonight, Farrah?"

Farrah shook her head. She should have known the moment she mouthed the word *bed* that Frank wouldn't waste time trying to get her into one. He'd been trying for a few years now and hadn't given up yet. The man just didn't get it, although she'd tried explaining it to him several times—and not even mincing her words while doing so. She thought her ex-husband had been scum, but Frank—who'd divorced his wife for the younger woman hired to nurse his wife after a near-fatal car accident—was no bargain either. Professionally, he was a skilled negotiator who deserved every penny of the six figures he made. As a man, he was as low on the totem pole as you could get. The only satisfaction she took was in knowing that eventually Frank's second wife had dumped him for a younger man, but not before cleaning out his bank account.

"Thanks, Frank, but I don't think so."

"Not this time?"

"Not ever."

"I won't give up."

"I wish you would," she threw over her shoulder as she moved toward the door. She was determined to prove she was just as stubborn as he was persistent.

"Will you continue to hate all men because of what your ex-husband did to you, Farrah?"

She continued walking, thinking his question didn't even deserve a response. She didn't hate all men because of Dustin. She just knew what she did or didn't want out of a relationship these days. Where she had once been the happily-ever-after kind of girl, the one who believed in white picket fences and everything that went along with it, she now knew that nothing was forever, especially a man's love. She refused to look at things through rose-colored glasses ever again.

A few moments later Farrah caught the elevator down to the lobby and exited the Stillwell Building to step out onto the busy sidewalk. She loved New York and thought there was no place quite like it. She tilted her head back to look up at all the tall buildings. Being here was always so invigorating.

Times Square. This was the heart of Manhattan. She could pick up the scent of fresh baked breads, see all the digital billboards flashing bright lights and watch people move so fast that if you didn't keep pace they would practically knock you over. For the few times a year she had to come here on business, she not only put up with it, she loved it.

Deciding not to take a cab since she wasn't too far from the hotel, she looked forward to a brisk walk. One of her coworkers had taken her out for a prime rib lunch. It was so scrumptious she'd even loaded the baked potato with butter and sour cream. She pushed guilt aside because this was December, the one month she ate whatever she wanted. She'd jump on the weight loss train like everyone else the first of the year. This was the season to be merry, so what were some extra calories now?

She thought about the case she would be working this week. She loved her job as a mediator at Holland and Bradford and couldn't imagine doing anything else. And as long as there were disputes to be ironed out, she would always be employed.

The reason her profession would remain in demand was because mediation was definitely less expensive than litigation, and in addition to the financial advantage, there was also the time saved. You didn't have to wait on court time, the worry of witnesses disappearing on you, or people not remembering facts occurring years before. Also, the sooner you could resolve a dispute, the sooner people's lives could get back to normal.

Lives getting back to normal...

A lot could be said for that, including hers. It had been six months since she and Xavier had ended things, and she was still trying to work him out of her system. It was as if she'd become addicted to the man. No matter how many times she'd washed her sheets, she couldn't get his scent out of them. After a while, she'd stopped trying and just went to bed each night breathing him in.

But that wasn't good because his scent reminded her of what they'd done between those sheets. She often dreamed about him, and in her dreams he did every single thing to her that he'd done while they'd been together and then some. More than once she had awakened the next morning with the covers tossed haphazardly on her bed and feeling like someone had ridden her all night. But that had only made her crave the real thing even more.

Breaking things off had been the right thing to do. She had begun anticipating his visits, wondering what he was up to during those days and nights he wasn't with her, getting antsy when he didn't call or acting like a bubbly sixteen-year-old when he did. Bottom line was that she had begun getting attached, and she'd sworn after Dustin that she would never get attached to another man again.

She tightened her coat around her, glad she'd worn boots because her toes were beginning to freeze. Seeing a wine shop ahead, she decided to stop in and make a purchase. There was nothing like a glass of wine to take the chill off. Besides, if it got too cold to venture out tomorrow, she would make good on what she'd told Frank. She'd stay in bed and enjoy the wine and the book she'd already purchased from a bookstore at the airport.

Farrah quickly opened the door to the wine shop and bumped into the person who was walking out. "Excuse me."

"No problem."

She snatched her head up. The sound of his voice and the scent of his cologne sent shock waves through her body. She gazed up into the man's dark eyes, recognizing them immediately. "Xavier!"

Chapter 2

It was quite obvious to Farrah that Xavier was as surprised to see her as she was to see him. Had it been six months since they'd last communicated? Six months since she'd had the best sex of her life?

She could remember, just as if it had been yesterday, the last time he had taken her—hard. And how the mouth she was staring at now had inflamed every single inch between her legs while she'd held on to his wide shoulders and cried out her pleasure.

She forced that thought from her mind, not wanting to go there, although her body was defying her and doing so anyway. As if on cue, the tips of her nipples felt sensitive against her blouse and a telltale ache was making itself known between her legs.

"What are you doing in New York?" she asked, and

then felt silly for doing so when she quickly recalled that Cody Enterprises had one of their offices here. Damn, he looked good, and seeing him again unnerved her, had her remembering just how he looked naked. He was wearing a full-length coat, but he didn't have to remove the coat for her to know the suit he wore looked as if it had been tailored just for him, and probably had been.

And there was his masculine physique—tall, well-built with a broad chest, massive shoulders and tapered thighs. Yes, she especially remembered those thighs. He worked out regularly at the gym which accounted for him being in such great shape. He was a man who took care of himself. He certainly had taken care of her.

"I'm here working. What about you?" he asked, as a smile touched his lips.

She wished he wouldn't smile. Seeing his mouth stretched wide was doing things to her. Making her remember other times he'd smiled at her and the reasons he'd done so. Like right after she'd licked him all over before taking him into her mouth.

"I'm working as a mediator for a case I've been assigned." She glanced down at the wine bottle in the bag he was carrying in his hand, and immediately knew what it meant. He was on his way to make a booty call. Whenever he'd done so with her, he'd always showed up with a bottle of wine. She remembered that oh, so well.

"How have you been?" she heard herself asking, glancing back up at him while fighting off anger at the thought he had probably reverted back to his old ways fairly easily, when she'd found it difficult to get back to hers. She hadn't slept with another man since him. The thought of doing so had turned her body off for some reason.

"I've been doing fine," he replied. "What about you?"

"Great. Just busy."

"Same here. How long will you be in New York?" he asked.

She wondered why he wanted to know. Did he not think this city was big enough for the both of them? That thought annoyed her. In fact, if she were to be honest with herself, she would admit to being annoyed with the whole split, although it had been her idea. A part of her hadn't expected him to agree to it so easily. When he'd left that night, not once had he looked back. She knew that for certain because she had watched him from her bedroom window until he'd gotten into his car and driven off.

According to her best friend, Natalie, who was married to Xavier's good friend Donovan, Xavier hadn't asked about her once. He could have, even if for no other reason than to inquire how she was doing. For all he'd known, she could have fallen off the face of the planet.

"I'm scheduled to fly out on Friday, but if the parties involved in the case don't reach a resolution by then, I'll be returning to New York sometime next week. At least I hope to return, but that will depend on the weather.

A snowstorm is supposed to be headed this way on Sunday," she said.

"So I heard, but I'll be here for another week, so if it does come, I'll be here with it."

Farrah nodded. "Well, I guess I'd better let you go. I wouldn't want you late for your date."

Too late she wished she could bite off her tongue. Had she just sounded like a jealous ex? She hoped not because it shouldn't matter one way or the other if he was on his way to see another woman.

"Who said I had a date?"

He asked the question in a deep, husky voice, which stirred something within her. She found the tone just as mesmerizing as his scent, which was all male. His signature cologne certainly knew how to make a woman hot and bothered. And then there was the way he was looking at her, with those gorgeous dark eyes of his, as if he knew he was making her panties wet.

She shrugged as she glanced back down at the wine bottle in the bag he was holding. "I just assumed you had one."

"I will if you'll have dinner with me."

She lifted a brow. "Dinner?"

"Yes. There are several restaurants around here. We can get caught up. I'd like to know how you've been doing since the last time I saw you."

He really didn't want to know, Farrah thought. He didn't need to know. It was best if they didn't go there. But, heaven help her, she would like to know what he'd been doing since the last time she saw him. "You sure you want to do that?"

"Why not? I see no reason why we shouldn't. I'd like to think, although we're no longer lovers, we're still friends."

Friends? Could two people go from being lovers to friends? After all, they'd shared a bed off and on for close to a year, longer than some people remained married.

She met his gaze, and the eyes looking deep into hers were robbing her of the ability to think straight. Instead she was overcome with memories of a satisfied woman, stretched out naked on a bed. And that woman was her. At least it had been her when they'd been together.

"So, since we're here in New York together, the least we can do is share dinner," he added in that resonant voice that could make her want to toss her panties to the wind any time and any place.

But then she knew that wasn't all he could make her toss to the wind. Her ability to resist his potent male charm topped the list. He already had the wine, so all he needed was a willing woman to share his bed…or for him to share hers.

Farrah drew in a deep breath as she thought about his invitation. Didn't she turn down Frank's invitation to dinner less than an hour ago? Why shouldn't she turn down this one as well? She really should, but for some reason, she couldn't fix her mouth to do that.

Going to dinner with him wouldn't be a big deal unless she made it one. And she wouldn't. She could handle it. And there was no reason why she couldn't handle him. He was just a man who'd been a past lover. And it was only dinner, and it didn't necessarily mean she would do anything foolish like sleep with him again. No way. No how.

"I'd love to join you for dinner, Xavier, but I'd like to go back to the hotel and change first."

"All right. What's the name of your hotel? I'll swing by and pick you up later. Let's say within the hour."

"I'm staying at the Waldorf Astoria."

She tried to ignore the flutter in her stomach when he smiled and said, "It's right up the street. Why don't I walk you there now and hang in the lobby while you change."

Farrah shook her head. "I can't ask you to do that. I'm sure you—"

"I don't mind waiting. I have some work I need to look over anyway," he said, lifting up his briefcase. "That would be easier than for me to go all the way to my home on Long Island and then come back," he added.

She knew in addition to the home he owned in Charlotte, he also had residences here in New York, Los Angeles and Florida. "You sure?" she asked.

"Positive."

"Okay, then, give me a minute to buy my wine."

"Sure."

At least he hadn't said anything about her sharing his, which meant after dinner there was still that possibility he would make one of his infamous booty calls to some woman. Why did she care? And why did the thought irk her?

She figured he would wait to the side for her to make her purchase. She hadn't counted on him following her when she walked up to the counter. And when he stood directly behind her, she could actually feel heat emanating from his body to hers. She was sure she'd felt it…or was she just imagining things?

She shook off the thought. Just the very idea that she had run into him—in New York of all places—was enough to torment her in one way and make her giddy in another. It wouldn't be so bad if she hadn't thought of him often. She had missed him, and although she would never admit such a thing to him, she would and could admit it to herself.

After making her purchase, she turned around to Xavier and smiled. "Thanks for waiting."

"No problem."

As they left the wine shop to head over to her hotel, she silently kept reminding herself that her days of lusting after Xavier had ended six months ago. Still, every time she felt his gaze on her she couldn't help but wonder if accepting his invitation to dinner had been a smart move after all.

Chapter 3

"I won't be long," Farrah said, giving Xavier a smile as she stepped on the elevator.

"Take your time. I'll be waiting down here in the lobby."

The elevator door slid shut, and it was only then that Xavier allowed himself a chance to breathe deeply. What were the odds of him running into the one woman he just couldn't seem to forget? And in New York of all places. A place that held memories for them both. At least they weren't back at the same hotel they'd been in for Donovan's wedding, he thought, settling down on one of the sofas in the lobby. Had that happened, it would have been one hell of a coincidence.

Still, just the thought of her going up to her room and taking off her clothes was doing all kinds of things to his libido…as if it wasn't out of whack already. The moment she'd bumped into him at that wine store and their bodies had touched, he had felt a frisson of heat consume him that could only be ignited by one woman. He'd known before looking into her face it was Farrah.

He settled back against the cushions of the sofa and recalled the last time they'd been in New York together, the first week in June for Donovan and Natalie's wedding. After the wedding he'd been invited to join Donovan's six cousins from Phoenix, his godbrothers as well as another good friend, Bronson Scott, for a night on the town. But the only night he'd wanted was in Farrah's bed, and as soon as the wedding reception had ended, he hadn't wasted any time going to her hotel room. And then a week later she had ended things between them.

Now they were both back in New York, and he would give anything for a repeat performance of what they'd shared the last time, although he knew doing so would be asking for trouble. And speaking of trouble, he pulled the cell phone from his pocket to call Beth to cancel his late night visit. He really didn't consider his time with Beth a "date," so he really hadn't lied to Farrah when she'd asked about it. As far as his mind and body were concerned, there was only one woman who had total control of his thoughts right now.

He leaned back and glanced around. This was a nice hotel, drenched in all kinds of history and decorated to the nines in elegance. He bet a lot of romantic trysts took place within these walls. He could see himself spending the night in one of those rooms upstairs if Farrah was so inclined. They would make love all night. He would make damn sure of it.

He reached down for his briefcase, and after placing it across his lap, he opened it up and pulled out a file. He might as well try to concentrate on something other than getting into Farrah's body and then hearing her scream after pumping her into an orgasm.

Moments later, after reading over several reports, he glanced beyond the huge glass doors and saw it had gotten dark outside already. He had a private car at his disposal twenty-four hours a day, but since the restaurant was just a block away there was no reason for them not to walk.

He closed his files, deciding to think about the eleven months he and Farrah had spent together after all, since his concentration was at an all-time low. She hadn't wanted a big deal made about their affair, so they hadn't made one. Although neither had announced it or flaunted it, he had been aware that his friends and hers suspected they were involved. But not at first.

Of course her best friend, Natalie, had known, which meant Donovan hadn't been clueless. And Cameron had known he was seeing some woman on a regular basis. His friend had never inquired as to whom, and Xavier had never openly shared the information.

His godbrothers—although they'd known he was sniffing real bad behind some woman—hadn't officially met her until Donovan's wedding. After that, they'd grilled him about why he'd gone to such pains to keep her a secret. And then he'd had to quickly spread the word at the wedding among the single men that she was taken after one of Donovan's cousins from Phoenix had tried hitting on her.

What he couldn't explain to anyone, least of all to himself, was the degree of possessiveness he felt toward Farrah. He'd felt the need to keep her all to himself and not share her or her time with anyone. Whenever he'd traveled on business, he'd found himself looking forward to returning to Charlotte to spend time with her. They had developed a routine and rarely ventured out beyond the walls of her house, preferring to remain inside—namely in the bedroom. That was the way they'd both wanted it. For some reason they'd enjoyed being detached from the outside world whenever they were together.

Showing up at her place, usually after eight at night, with his bottle of wine, had become the norm whenever he was in town, and they would often joke about it. He knew the wine was the reason she'd figured he was about to make a booty call tonight, and she had been right.

But what Farrah didn't know was that he hadn't been sexually involved with a woman since her, and Beth would have only been a substitute for the one woman he truly wanted. The woman he was sitting in the lobby waiting for at that very moment.

As if he conjured her, the elevator door opened, and Farrah stepped out. He blinked as he stared at her. She was wearing a long coat so he couldn't see her outfit, but just seeing her made his erection spring to life. He was grateful his briefcase was still placed across his lap, and he kept it strategically placed in front of him when he stood, trying to get control of his mind and body.

"You look nice, Farrah," he said, reaching for his coat on the sofa beside him.

"Thanks. If you'd like, you can leave your briefcase and wine at the front desk until we return, or I can take it back up to my room," she said sliding her hands into a pair of black leather gloves.

He preferred her taking it back up to her room so he'd have an excuse to go up there when they got back. Or he could go back up to her room with her now to leave the items. But if he were to follow her up to her hotel room, that would be asking for trouble. Seeing Farrah made him realize just how much he'd missed her. How much he still wanted her.

"I can leave them at the front desk. That's no problem," he heard himself saying, knowing that was the best option.

"You sure?"

Yes, he was sure—if she wanted to keep her clothes on for the rest of the night. "Yes, I'm sure. Ready to go?"

She nodded. "Yes."

Together they strolled over to the front desk, and he completed a claim slip for his belongings. Moments later they were walking through the hotel's glass door to exit the building. The temperature had dropped dramatically, and the cold air seemed to blast down on them the moment they stepped onto the sidewalk.

"Wow, it's freezing out here," Farrah said, tightening her leather coat around her.

Instead of responding, on instinct Xavier wrapped his arms around her waist to bring her closer to his side. The moment he touched her, a shot of something akin to hot liquid fire exploded through his veins and he nearly groaned out loud. But he kept his arms around her to share his heat, grateful for his own wool coat. However, nothing could stop his reaction to the feel of her being plastered to his body.

That made him remember how it was being skin to skin with her while they made love, sliding in and out of her body, feeling her moist heat clench him in a way that could make him moan out her name.

She didn't look over at him. Instead she stared straight ahead. He didn't have a problem with that; in fact, he much preferred it. If their gazes were to connect now, he would be tempted to take her mouth and to tongue her right in the middle of the sidewalk.

He decided talking would be much safer, so he asked, "Warmer now?"

She nodded. "Yes and thanks. We have cold weather back in Charlotte, but this seems to be a different kind of cold. I'm even wearing an extra layer of clothing."

Telling him what she had on her body wasn't helping matters, he thought, especially when he was having visions of her not wearing anything at all. He always enjoyed seeing her naked. But then her clothing was known to be sexy as well. He recalled arriving one night when she'd worked late at the office and she'd been wearing a two-piece suit. She'd looked professional as well as sensual.

Even now he couldn't help wondering what she was wearing underneath her long coat. All he could see was a nice pair of chocolate-colored suede boots.

"Is the restaurant far?" she interrupted his thoughts to ask.

He smiled, hearing the shiver in her voice. His woman was cold. He frowned. He'd never thought of any female as "his woman" before. That had definitely been a slip of the senses.

"No, in fact it's right on the corner. Otherwise, I would have called for a car. However, I did call ahead and make reservations while you were upstairs getting dressed."

"Good. I could eat a horse about now."

And he could eat her. Pushing that thought out of his mind, he tried dwelling on what she said. One of the things he'd always liked about Farrah was that she had no problems filling her plate with the takeout he'd bring with him to her place. How she managed to stay in such fantastic shape was beyond him. She had the kind of curves that would make any man take a second look and moan, then take another look and wish.

"Here we are," he said, opening the door to the Chinese restaurant. He knew how much she enjoyed Asian foods and had immediately remembered this place. He had eaten here a few months ago while in New York on business and had thought of her then. But to be honest, he'd thought of her a lot since they'd ended things between them.

"Nice place," she said, glancing around.

He followed her gaze. Like them, several couples had braved the cold temperatures to eat out this evening.

After providing the hostess their names, they followed the woman to an area in the back where a fireplace had a blaze roaring, emitting plenty of heat. He assisted Farrah in removing her coat to hang it up on a nearby rack. When he saw her outfit, his heart began pounding in his chest and his body tightened in ways only she could make it do.

She was wearing a short tan-colored wool skirt, brown tights and a multicolor V-neck cardigan sweater. The way the sweater draped over her skirt emphasized her small waist and those nice curves he'd been thinking about earlier. His gaze traveled the full length of her physique, from the curly shoulder length hair, past a well-endowed chest, down her thighs and to shapely legs encased in a pair of knee-high boots.

While removing her gloves, she seemed not to notice the way he was staring at her. A muscle jerked in his jaw as he watched her slide into her chair. He felt sort of off balance, and he realized the depth of his desires for this particular woman was...well, getting exposed. Trying to get a grip, he moved away slightly to remove his own coat and proceeded to place it on the rack next to Farrah's before taking the chair across from her.

"How did you find out about this place?" she asked,

smiling, while picking up the menu a waitress placed in front of them.

He met her gaze, and a sensual shiver ran through him. He had been attracted to her from the first time they met, and over a year later he was still very much attracted to her now. "Cameron and I came here for a business meeting in September. Like you, he enjoys Chinese food, and not surprisingly, he knew about this place."

She nodded. "And how is Mr. Cody doing these days? Natalie mentioned Vanessa's pregnant and they're expecting a baby in the spring."

Since Vanessa was Donovan's cousin, Xavier was aware Farrah had met Vanessa at a bridal shower given for Natalie last spring, but Farrah hadn't met Cameron until the wedding.

"Cameron is fine, and yes, Vanessa is due in April, and they already know it's going to be a little girl. He's excited about that. I can see her wrapping her dad around her little finger."

During one of their pillow talk sessions, he'd told her a lot about Cameron, and how their friendship began back at Harvard. He'd even shared with her how determined his friend had been to win Vanessa Steele's love.

"It seems strange," Farrah said, taking a sip of her water.

He arched a brow. "What does?"

"Being here with you. This is the first time we've ever gone out on a real date."

She was right. By mutual consent, they hadn't had that kind of relationship. From the beginning, they'd only wanted one thing from each other—a good time in bed.

"First time for everything," he said, studying his own menu and dismissing her observation as nothing more than that and not a complaint.

"I know, but it just seems strange."

He decided not to tell her what really seemed strange was them *sitting* at a table, instead of him having her naked body spread across it and eager to have her for his meal, or getting ready to thrust into her. Xavier shifted in his seat at the memories of both and felt his persistent erection press hard against his zipper.

He would be the first to admit he'd considered asking her out on a number of occasions but had changed his mind. He'd known from the get-go that she had a problem with any type of serious involvement, and although she'd never really gone into details as to what her ex-husband had done that had resulted in the breakup of her marriage, he'd gotten the lowdown anyway from Donovan, who'd gotten it from Natalie. And just thinking about what the man had done to her filled him with anger. No man should hurt a woman the way her ex had hurt her, and on that same note, no woman should intentionally use a man the way Dionne had used him.

"See anything you like?"

He glanced over at her. It was on the tip of his tongue to tell her that yes, he saw what he liked and she was sitting across from him. There was so much about her he'd enjoyed during the months they'd shared a relationship. Even now he would love to go back to her place or take her to his and make love to her like he used to do, all night long.

There was something about being inside of her that would often make him pound into her almost nonstop, never to cause pain, only intense pleasure for the both of them. And during those times when she'd locked her hot lips around his shaft, gently scraping her teeth across his most sensitive flesh, his pleasure had been almost unbearable.

He picked up his cold glass of water and took a huge gulp, appreciating how good it felt flowing down his throat to cool his heated insides. But that only lasted for a little while. All it took was a glance over at her, to see the creamy brown texture of her skin, the long lashes fanning her dark brown eyes, the high cheekbones with a dimple in each and the shape of her mouth to know even after their separation, he was still very much in lust with her.

"Xavier?"

He then realized that he hadn't answered. "Yes. I think I'm going to try the pepper steak with onions and white rice. I had it the last time I was here and thought it was good." *But not as good as you,* he thought to himself. *Nothing is as good as you.*

"That sounds like a winner and I think I'll have that, too."

Moments later, after placing their order with the waitress, Farrah settled back in her chair recalling what had filled her mind when Xavier had removed his coat. His tall, muscular frame always excited her whether he was in a suit or a pair of jeans. Business or casual wear, it didn't matter. He exuded an air of total masculinity in anything he put on his body.

And then there were his facial features—definite eye candy of the sweetest kind. His strong, sensuous jaw, full lips, sculpted nose and chocolate brown eyes. And the dimple in his left cheek, she thought, added the finishing touch.

What she'd told Xavier earlier was true. Being with him, sitting across from each other in a restaurant, felt strange mainly because they'd never actually gone out on a date before. Their relationship had been defined from the beginning. She'd told him the night they'd met at the Racetrack Café that the last thing she wanted was an involvement in a serious relationship. She'd been there and done that with her marriage and had no intentions of doing so again.

She had explained, and quite specifically, that all she wanted was an occasional bed partner, a lover who wouldn't get underfoot and become possessive and be a nuisance. She wanted a man who would know and understand the only rights he was entitled to were the ones she gave him.

Xavier had agreed to her terms without batting an eye because his wants and desires from a relationship had been identical to hers. She didn't know the whole story, since it hadn't been her business to ask him. But out of curiosity she had asked Natalie, who had heard what had happened from Donovan. It seemed some chick in college, whom he'd fallen in love with, had done him in, and as a result he'd erected a stone wall around his heart. Probably similar to the stone wall she had around her own.

From the first, they'd gotten along marvelously. Since they both traveled a lot in their professions, there had been times when they hadn't seen each other for weeks. That hadn't bothered her since she appreciated her space and didn't like overcrowding of any kind. He had, however, on occasion given her a call during those times to see how she was doing. She merely took those as him being thoughtful and nothing more. She had never returned the gesture, although he had given her his business card with all his contact information.

For some reason, she'd never felt inclined to hold a conversation with him outside of their pillow talk. It was only then, while her body had been recuperating from the effects of mind-blowing orgasms, that he had shared things about himself. He'd never said a whole lot, just enough to let her know he was an okay guy who didn't have a lot of the issues that some men did. He had learned from his past mistakes the same way she had learned from hers. Emotional involvements weren't what they were cracked up to be and were best left alone.

He had told her about his five godbrothers and the story of how their fathers had made a pact upon graduating from college. She'd met them at Donovan and Natalie's wedding and thought they were really nice guys and admired their close friendship.

"So tell me about the case you're here working on, Farrah."

The sound of his sexy voice made her glance up, and immediately she wished she hadn't. Intentional or not, he had a look in his eyes that stirred desire she hadn't felt since the last time she'd seen him. The last time she'd shared a bed with a man. Just remembering made the area between her thighs ache like crazy.

She shifted in her seat before saying, "What I have are best friends from high school who started a cosmetics company together after college." She filled him in on the details of the case, then explained, "The new husband wants her to sell her share at what the other partner sees as an outlandish amount since she hadn't been involved in the day-to-day operations of the business."

Xavier nodded. "Doesn't matter. If she's still listed as a partner, whether she contributed to the success of the company or not, she's entitled to her share, usually a fifty-fifty split, unless it can be proven that such an oral agreement was made."

Farrah couldn't stop the smile that touched her lips. "Everything you've said might be true from a legal standpoint, but I'm a mediator and not an attorney. My concern is not who is right or wrong in this case. My job is to facilitate a process of resolution, to help them work through the issue and resolve it."

"You enjoy your work?" He realized he'd never asked her that before.

"Um, I find it rewarding. The people I deal with

usually can come to an amicable decision on most issues and I like helping them get there," she said.

At that moment the waitress returned with their food, which Xavier felt was timely since it gave him a chance to ponder all the things he didn't know about her, despite having been involved in an affair with her for almost a year. He'd known the basics—like what she did for a living, her marital status and that her parents were divorced and she'd been an only child. He'd also known from observation that she was an extremely neat person, which he could appreciate since he was as well.

"What about you, Xavier? Do you enjoy your work?"

He glanced over at her. Just as he'd never inquired about her work, she'd never inquired about his until now. Once in a while after making love, he would share things with her, just for conversational purposes, nothing more. "Pretty much, although some days are more hectic than others. Cam keeps me busier than any of my other clients, but he's pretty good to work for."

"I'd think being a counselor for someone who is also a close friend would be hard."

He chuckled. "It's not hard because we try and keep it real. My job is to protect his interests and he knows I have his back and will give him the best advice. It's all about trust."

They didn't say anything for a while as they ate their food, but he couldn't help wondering what she was thinking. Was she thinking that going on a date with him wasn't so bad and perhaps they should do it again? He didn't have a problem with it if she didn't.

"This is good."

He glanced over at her and saw the smile on her face. "I'm glad you think so."

Xavier resumed eating and tried to get out of his mind how good she looked. She'd always looked good before, but today she looked even better. It might just be his mind messing with him since he hadn't seen or talked to her in a while.

"So what have you been up to lately?" she asked.

He glanced up again and watched as she put food in her mouth and began chewing. Damn, she even turned him on just by chewing her food.

He dropped his gaze to his plate to gain control of his senses before lifting them again to her. "I've been doing a lot of international traveling, mostly to the Middle East."

"The Middle East?"

"Yes, a country call Mowaiti. Natalie might have mentioned that one of her cousin in-laws, Quade Westmoreland, has a cousin who is married to a sheikh."

"She did. I met Cheyenne at one of Natalie's bridal showers and got to meet Quade at the wedding. They have adorable triplets."

He smiled. "Quade introduced Cameron to Sheikh Jamal Yasir, and they're discussing a possible joint business venture in Dubai. I had to be on hand during those talks."

Farrah flashed him another smile. "Cameron is definitely a mover and a shaker, isn't he?"

"Yes, he is."

She would probably be surprised to know that Xavier thought she was a mover and a shaker as well. She had certainly moved his libido up a monumental notch since knowing her, and she was shaking his common sense right out of his head, making him think of all kinds of naughty things he'd like to do to her. He wondered what her response would be if he were to ask to share her bed tonight. For old times' sake.

He drew in a deep breath, knowing that doing something like that wasn't a good idea. Their relationship had ended months ago, the decision mutually accepted by both, and they'd moved on. Or had they? She seemed to have handled the split well, and on his good days, he thought so had he. But now he wasn't so sure.

He was definitely due for a cold shower when he got home. But as he continued to watch her eat, getting turned on every time she took a bite of her food, he knew that a cold shower wouldn't put an end to what he was feeling or the raw, primitive need growing inside of him.

And he would be the first to admit that that wasn't good.

Xavier Kane will not break down my defenses tonight!

Those words echoed in Farrah's head while she buttoned her coat after dinner. The meal had been more than delicious, and the conversation between them enjoyable. Her misgivings regarding the breaking down of her defenses could have been put to rest if sometime during the course of dinner, she could have stopped remembering certain things.

Every time Xavier had picked up his wine glass to take a sip and planted his mouth on the rim of the glass, she could recall him planting his mouth on certain parts of her body just that way. Xavier had a way with his mouth that surpassed that of any man she'd ever known. And now that they were about to leave the toasty warm haven of the restaurant, she needed the strength not to succumb to those memories and give him the idea that she wanted more than the dinner they'd just shared.

"Ready?" he asked after she worked her hand into the remaining glove.

She glanced up at him and met his gaze, saw the look that flashed in the dark depths of his eyes and had to compose herself quickly. He wanted her. She had seen that look many times before, and although it had flared to life in his gaze just for an instant, it had been there. The impact of that sudden and unexpected look had her pulling in a deep breath.

She was well aware that Xavier would follow her lead. He was a man who only took what was offered. There was no doubt in her mind if she gave him even the slightest indication that she reciprocated that desire, he would pounce on it. Pounce on her. Umm, the thought of him pouncing, especially on her, wasn't a bad one.

She smiled, fighting back the urge to ask if he was interested in going back to her hotel and making love to her all night long. "Yes, I'm ready to leave, although I'm not ready for what I know is awaiting me outside that door," she finally said. "I feel a chill in my bones already, just thinking about how cold it is. And I'm sure the temperature has dropped some more since we got here."

He chuckled. "It probably has. Would it make you feel better if I promise to keep you warm?"

Depends on how you go about accomplishing it, she quickly thought. It wasn't an impossible feat where he was concerned, especially since he had the ability to set her on fire whenever and however he chose to do so. "Yes, that will certainly make me feel better," she said.

"Then I'll make you that promise," he said engulfing her gloved hand in his. The glove was no buffer from the power of his touch, and automatically, sensations began swirling around in the pit of her stomach and sliding down to the lower part of her body. They were invading her feminine core and making her crave things she was better off not having—especially from the man standing in front of her looking like he could eat her alive if given the chance.

And it was a chance she refused to give him, no matter how much she was tempted. She knew now the same thing she'd known six months ago, the same thing she'd discovered the night of Natalie and Donovan's wedding reception when he'd given her the best sex of her life. Four orgasms later—or had it been five?—she'd finally reached the conclusion that after sharing his bed for nearly a year, he was the one man who could make her think of losing her heart again. And it was a heart she'd guarded, protected and shielded since being dumped by Dustin.

She decided now not to comment on his promise. Since she'd learned from experience never to trust a promise from a man, she merely smiled as he led her out of the restaurant. The moment they exited the door, a cold blast of winter air smacked her face, and she couldn't help but grin when she saw a private car waiting at the curb.

She glanced up at Xavier. "Your car and driver, right?"

"Yes."

"But how did he know to come here?" she asked.

"I called him while you were in the ladies room. He had to come pick me up anyway, so I figured he could very well do it here. It would save us the bother of walking back to your hotel in the cold. I promised to keep you warm."

And then before she could catch her next breath, she was swept off her feet into a pair of strong arms. "Xavier! What are you doing?"

"Carrying you to the car to make sure you don't slip."

She couldn't resist burying her nose for a quick second in his chest. Her face may have touched wool material, but her nose inhaled the scent of a man. A man who used to be the best lover she'd ever had.

His driver opened the door, and Xavier deposited her on the backseat of the car with the ease of a man who knew just how to take care of a woman, and she knew that he did.

She scooted over when he slid in beside her, but not for long. The moment the driver closed the door, he pulled her against his side.

"Thanks, Xavier. You didn't have to do that," she said removing her gloves and placing them in the pocket of her coat.

"Yes, I did," he said, reaching out and letting his fingertips stroke the side of her face. "I like taking care of you, Farrah."

His words oozed liquid heat that sizzled along her nerve endings. She tilted her head to look up at him, and he stared back, watching her with an expression that turned the sizzle into a flame and sent shudders racing through her. How had he managed to do that with just a look?

She knew the answer before the question fully blossomed in her mind. It was there in the darkness of his gaze, a red-hot hunger that had the ability to strip her control, eradicate her resistance and make her crave the kind of pleasure that only Xavier Kane could deliver.

"Xavier." She heard herself moan his name, unable to hold it back any longer. And while she continued to watch him, taking in how his lashes fanned over the intensity of his dark gaze and how his lips formed a curve like they always did right before he got ready to devour her mouth, she felt a deep need spiral between her thighs.

She was tumbling into forbidden territory and

couldn't stop herself. He was there, but he wouldn't lift one finger to keep her from falling. She knew that. In fact, he was poised, ready to push her over the edge if he had to. But she couldn't let that happen, not for her peace of mind and her survival.

However, what she could do and what she would allow was a way to satisfy them both for a little while. A kiss. They could even turn their kiss into a full make-out session. It would be a quick moment of satisfaction, but it would be well worth it, she told herself. No harm, right?

How could tangling her tongue with his cause any harm as long as it didn't lead to anything? She convinced herself that it wouldn't as she eased her body closer to his on the leather seat. She felt his finger move from her face to the back of her neck and begin stroking her there. Her body automatically responded to his touch.

When he lowered his head and met her lips, she heard herself groan in a way that only he could make her do. And she knew before it was over she would do more than moan.

Chapter 4

Xavier felt as if he'd come home the moment his tongue invaded Farrah's mouth. It was as if he had been away from his favorite place and was returning to a hometown welcome of the most sensuous kind.

He relished the taste of her with a primitive longing and with an urgency he couldn't deny. Not that he was thinking about denying it. He didn't intend to leave any part of her mouth untouched, untapped or unstroked. He loved her taste. He had missed it. And he was damn near starving for it.

He was kissing her with an intensity he felt in every part of his body, including the erection that nearly burst his zipper. Only Farrah had the ability to make him want to toss caution to the wind, say the hell with it and take her as he pleased. There had been so many times he had ached to take her without wearing a condom, wanting the feel of her flesh clenching him instead of the latex separating them.

And now it wouldn't take much for him to take her right here. His driver, Jules, had had the good sense to use the privacy shield and was probably driving around Manhattan at his leisure since he was certain they would have been back to Farrah's hotel by now.

The backseat of the car was dark and intimate and had the scent of pure woman. She was kissing him back with an intensity that matched his own, and the way she was sucking deep on his tongue was bringing to life every erotic bone in his body. She tasted hot, untamed, and he knew they were both on the verge of unleashing sensations they had kept bottled up for too long.

She pulled her mouth away and drew in a deep breath, evidently needing to breathe. Personally, he needed more of her taste, but would give her a moment. He watched as she glanced out of the car window. Although they could see out of it, no one could see them inside because of the window's darkened tint. "Where are we?" she asked.

Xavier smiled, refusing to remove his hand from her neck, liking the feel of the soft skin his fingertips were stroking. He curved his hand around her neck even more, making sure she didn't try easing away from him. "Driving around the city."

She glanced back at him and smiled. "On a sightseeing tour?"

He returned her smile. "If that's what *Jules* wants to think, but I think we know better, don't we?"

"Yes."

And then he reached out and lifted her out of the seat and into his lap and captured her mouth once again.

Farrah wrapped her arms around Xavier's neck while he continued to plunder her mouth with a hunger that had her moaning again. She wasn't sure how long the ride would last, but she planned to take advantage of every tormenting and satisfying minute.

Even through his coat she could feel the hardness of his erection poking her in the backside, but she didn't mind. In fact, she relished the feel and regretted that clothing separated their bodies.

Evidently he felt the same way when he released the back of her neck, and his fingers went to the buttons of her coat while his tongue was still inside her mouth. She wanted him so bad she was almost consumed by the mere idea of being here, in the backseat of a car in his lap while he kissed her senseless. His tongue was teasing and tormenting her into sweet oblivion, and there was nothing she could do about it. There was nothing she wanted to do about it.

She felt him spread open her coat before his fingers went about tackling the buttons of her cardigan. She knew this was lust of the most potent kind, and it was probably time for her to rein him back in, but when he eased free a button and touched a spot above her bra, she could do nothing but moan.

He knew what touching her breasts did to her, and she had a feeling he was about to get downright naughty.

And when he eased open the next button, she knew she was right.

She pulled her mouth away from his. "Xavier?"

"Umm?" he asked, taking the tip of his tongue and licking the area around her chin.

"What are you doing?" She knew it was a stupid question, but she asked it anyway. It was quite obvious that he was seducing her.

"Letting you know how much I've missed you."

That was definitely the wrong answer because she knew, although she would never admit it, that she'd missed him, too.

"I think I've gotten the message," she said in a soft tone when he released yet another button.

He tilted his head and met her gaze. "Not sure you have yet and not to the degree that I want you to know," he said in a deep, husky voice. "By the time you get back to your hotel room tonight, there will be no doubt in your mind just how much I've truly missed you, Farrah."

That meant he planned to torture her some more, probably a whole lot more, before it was all over. How far would he go? How far would she let him? Those questions slipped from her mind when her cardigan opened, exposing her lace bra to his view. She knew blue was his favorite color. Had she worn a blue bra for that reason tonight? And one with a front clasp?

He released the front hook, and her body began vibrating in pleasure when he lowered his head to take a hardened nipple into his mouth. "Xavier." She whimpered his name on a breathless sigh and grabbed ahold of his head. Not to push him away but to keep his mouth right there to feast on her.

Shudders tore into her, touching every part of her body, tearing at nerve endings with every stroke of his tongue on her nipple. She tightened her legs, feeling a throb between them so deep she wanted to scream. She was on the verge of one hell of an explosion. She knew it, and from her past history, he had to know it as well.

It didn't take penetration to make her come. Xavier's mouth anywhere on her was known to do the trick. She had a feeling this would be one of those times, because tonight he was being generous *and* naughty, a combination that could cost her. At that moment, though, nothing seemed more important than having him suck her nipples like he was doing now.

Unless he decided he wanted to...

The thought of his tongue sliding between her womanly folds had her releasing a trembling breath, and when she felt his hand work its way under her skirt to touch a thigh, she couldn't help but groan out loud. She needed to get laid and bad. The hot ache between her thighs was all but demanding it, and the mouth planted firmly on her breast seconded that motion.

"We've reached the Waldorf Astoria, Mr. Kane."

The sound of the driver's voice was a colder blast than the one she'd felt when they'd walked out of the restaurant. Why now, when she'd been so close to her body fragmenting in one sensuous explosion? Talk about lousy timing.

She looked up and met Xavier's gaze and knew he was thinking the same thing. She also knew what else he was thinking…

Farrah drew in a deep breath and watched as he palmed delicately over her breasts before he began refastening her bra. "Circle the block one more time, Jules," he said.

"Just one block, sir?"

"Yes."

By the time the vehicle began moving again, a semblance of Farrah's common sense had returned. But the part still lurking out there in Blissville had her worried because she was fully aware just what an orgasm at the hands and mouth of Xavier Kane could mean. She would sleep well tonight and wake up tomorrow probably craving even more.

She knew she had to regain control and not succumb to a weakness of the body nor a deep addiction for him. When he had buttoned her sweater and pulled the lapels of her coat together, he met her gaze. And then while she was still nestled snugly in his lap, he lowered his head and kissed her again.

This kiss had all the intensity of the last, probably more so, and she could only kiss him back while shudders shook her from head to toe. When he finally released her mouth moments later, it was on the tip of that same tongue he'd just ravished to ask him up to her room for a nightcap, although they would both know the true intent of the invitation.

But a part of her kept from doing so. It was the part

that couldn't forget or let go of the pain she'd felt the day Dustin had asked for a divorce to marry another woman.

"I got my bottle of wine and you have yours," Xavier said softly close to her moist lips. "How about if we…"

"Drink them separately," she finished for him.

He leaned back, lifted a brow and was probably as surprised as she that she wasn't inviting him up to her room. She would probably hate herself later, and the area between her legs would probably protest something awful, but that area of her chest where her heart was planted would eventually thank her for sparing it from further damage. It had finally gotten repaired, and she refused to let it get broken again.

"You sure you want that, Farrah?"

She decided to answer him the only way she knew how. Honestly. "No, that's not what I want, but I know that's what I need to happen, Xavier. For my sake, you're going to have to trust me on this."

He opened his mouth to say something, and then as if he thought better of it, he clamped his mouth shut. He brought her hand to his face and gently rubbed against it. "Leaving you alone tonight isn't going to be easy, Farrah," he said in a low, sexy voice.

"And having you leave me alone won't be easy, Xavier. But for my peace of mind, I don't have a choice. Please say you understand, or please try to."

He met her gaze and held it for a long moment. And then a slow smile of understanding tugged at his sensuous lips. "I'll try, but only if you agree to see me again while you're here."

"What's the point?" she couldn't help but ask.

He cupped her chin in his hand. "To prove I'm not a bad guy."

She shook her head. "I never thought you were a bad guy, Xavier. If I had thought that, you would not have shared my bed. In fact, I think you're too good to be true and that's what scares me."

"Too good to be true?"

"Yes, both physically and emotionally. I could end up getting hurt. You wouldn't hurt me intentionally, but I could get hurt just the same and I can't let that happen."

She knew she had said too much, had let her feelings become raw and exposed, but he needed to understand and accept what she was saying. He was becoming the one weakness she had to do without.

When Jules opened the car door for them, he slid out, and before her leg could touch the sidewalk, he had whisked her into his arms again. "Xavier!"

Jules raced ahead to open the glass door to the hotel, and Xavier didn't place her back on her feet until they stood in the hotel's lobby.

"I need to get my items from the front desk," he said. "But first I'll walk you to the elevator."

He tucked her hand in his and they walked toward the elevator. "I'll call you tomorrow, Farrah. I'd like to take you to a Broadway play while you're here."

"Xavier, I—"

He placed a finger to her lips. "At least think about it. It will be just two friends going out. No big deal."

She drew in a deep breath. *No big deal? Yeah, right.* She'd assumed going to dinner with him tonight would not be a big deal either, but it turned out to be one anyway. "I'll see if I'm available."

"All right."

He leaned down and brushed a kiss across her lips when the elevator door opened. She stepped inside and glanced over her shoulder at him. "Good night, Xavier."

"Good night, Farrah."

And as the elevator carried her from the lobby up to her room, she couldn't help wondering how she was going to turn him down when he called her tomorrow.

Chapter 5

"Good morning, Mr. Kane."

"Good morning, Vicki. Hold my calls for a while. By the way, you look nice this morning."

Xavier entered his office thinking his secretary's attire, a beige pantsuit, looked more appropriate for the office than those sexy outfits she'd been wearing. He was glad she'd taken his advice.

He eased out of his jacket and then sat down in the chair behind his desk. He was ready to roll his sleeves up and get some work done. He hadn't been sure he would ever get to sleep last night, but when he had finally done so, he had basically slept like a baby. But that hadn't kept visions of a hot and ready Farrah out of his mind. At least that's how she used to be. This overly cautious Farrah would take some getting used to.

His cell phone rang and he leaned forward to pull it off his belt. "Yes?"

"When are you returning to Charlotte, X?"

He smiled at the sound of Uriel Lassiter's voice. Since he and his five godbrothers had been kids, they'd shortened each other's names to just the first letter. "Why you want to know? You miss me, U?"

"No. It's Ellie."

Xavier chuckled. "Your wife misses me?"

"No, and stop being a smart ass. Ellie's having a New Year's Eve party and wants to make sure you're coming, especially since no one knows your schedule for the holidays."

He leaned back in his chair. "I still haven't decided where I'll be for Christmas but I'm game for New Year's. And as far as when I'll be returning to Charlotte, it will depend on how soon we can close the deal here. I hope to be back in Charlotte in a week."

"And then you're taking the rest of the month off, right?"

"That's right."

"Good. Z is coming home."

Xavier sat up straight in his chair, surprised. "He is?"

"Yes. I talked to him last night." Uriel chuckled. "He couldn't tell Ellie no, so he'll be here for Christmas and New Year's."

Xavier nodded. Of his five godbrothers, Zion was the youngest, at twenty-eight, and the most well-known because of the jewelry he designed. And he was the one who at the moment was going through some major issues. Before she died four years ago, his mother had revealed to him that she wasn't sure that the man Zion thought was his father really was since she'd taken a lover during the earlier part of her marriage.

It was Zion's secret, one he'd only shared with his godbrothers. Xavier figured it would be an easy enough thing to prove or disprove, but Zion didn't want to risk his father ever finding out that the woman he'd loved so much had once been unfaithful to him. So instead of hanging around and letting something slip, Zion had escaped to Rome and built a home and an empire there. Xavier couldn't help wondering if Z had finally figured you can't run away from your problems and was now thinking about moving back to the States.

Moments later, Xavier was hanging up the phone and pulling a file off the huge stack of papers on his desk. His thoughts, however, shifted to Farrah, and he couldn't help but remember what she'd said about not wanting to get hurt again. He knew how she felt. Wasn't that the same reason he'd avoided serious involvement with women?

What he needed to do was prove they could enjoy themselves without getting all that serious. They had done so for close to a year, so there was no reason they couldn't continue. After such a long separation, he was certain if they rekindled their affair, they would be mindful of the mistakes they had begun making the last time by getting too attached.

The thought of them falling in love was scary stuff.

He knew that better than anyone. But he was just as certain it wouldn't happen. There wasn't a woman alive he would give his heart to. He had no intention of getting great sex confused with any emotions of the heart. Things didn't work that way for him, and he was sure things wouldn't work that way for her either.

Her ex had damaged her emotionally on the institution of marriage, so what was the problem? Why couldn't two people who only wanted to enjoy off-the-chain sex do so without worrying about their hearts getting in the way?

It would be up to him to convince her that they could resume their no-strings-attached affair with no entanglements, and he intended to do just that.

"Mrs. Byers and Ms. Shaw, we're here to bring about an acceptable resolution to the case pending before Judge Lewis Braille. Hopefully, we'll reach an agreeable resolution so that we can avoid a costly court battle and—"

"Not unless that woman gives my wife her fair share of what is due to her."

Farrah frowned at Mr. Byers's outburst. She'd known the moment he'd walked into the room with his wife that he was bad news. For some reason, he thought he was calling the shots. He might very well do so in his marriage, but she had no intention of letting him take control of these proceedings.

"Mr. Byers, I need you to refrain from speaking out of turn. Doing so will not get us anywhere."

"Please calm down, Rudolph," Lori Byers whispered to her husband in a calm voice. "Please let Ms. Langley do her job so we won't have to go to court."

Other than a roll of her eyes, Kerrie Shaw didn't say anything, although it was evident she was angry at what Rudolph Byers had said.

When the parties had entered the room, Farrah's keen sense of observation had picked up on several points. Even with all this legal mess going on, it was plain to see that the two women had shared a very close friendship at one time, and if given the chance, without any outside interference, that friendship could be restored.

It was also quite obvious they still cared for each other. That was probably the reason Kerrie Shaw had refrained from speaking her mind a few moments ago when Mr. Byers had spoken out of line. Farrah figured she'd kept her mouth closed to spare Lori Byers's feelings. That meant during the time they'd been friends, Kerrie had had the role of protector, and Lori had been the one more vulnerable and easily swayed and misled.

Farrah glanced over at Rudolph and quickly decided that was exactly what was taking place now. Lori allowed the man she had fallen in love with to come between her and her friend. Their close relationship had started in high school and continued in college and through Lori's first marriage and birth of her two little girls. Lori had even named Kerrie as godmother for her two girls.

Both women were now thirty-four. Kerrie was engaged to be married and Lori's first husband had been killed in a car accident a few years ago. She had met Rudolph on the internet, which didn't say a whole lot to some, but definitely spoke volumes to Farrah. Not that all pickups from cyberspace were bad, but the one Farrah had landed a couple of years ago, Alvin Cornell, had made her want to toss him right back. He'd been such a jerk. She could only wonder if Alvin had an older brother by the name of Rudolph.

How two women who had been such good friends could let a man come between them was beyond Farrah. She couldn't imagine any man or woman coming in and destroying her and Natalie's friendship, which had been in existence since high school as well. After her breakup with Dustin, it had been Natalie who'd been there for her, to help her get through the worst time in her life. Natalie had known she would wallow in self-pity her first Christmas as a divorced woman and had flown into Charlotte from New Jersey to spend time with her so she wouldn't be alone, and to make her see there was life after divorce.

"Yes, let's continue," Farrah said in an authoritative voice, more so for Rudolph Byers's benefit than for the two women. "As I was saying, my goal is to resolve the complaint and conflict informally. I'm impartial. I don't know either of you, and have no ties, previous or present, to your company."

Farrah paused and then looked back and forth at the women. "My concern is not who is right. It doesn't matter to me. I'm here to work you through this, and in doing that you need to talk to me about why you think you were wronged and how we can resolve things and move forward. Are there any questions?"

"No," both women said simultaneously.

Farrah noted Rudolph had clenched down on his lips to keep from answering, but the glare he gave her let her know he wanted to say something. Probably something he had no business saying.

"I hope we can work things out," Lori said softly. "I don't want anger between me and Kerrie."

"Who cares if there's anger between the two of you?" Rudolph butted in to say, evidently not able to keep quiet any longer. "I won't let her sell that company without giving you every penny you deserve."

Farrah drew in a deep breath and shifted her gaze to Kerrie. She could tell it was taking all Kerrie's control to not lash out against Rudolph, and she knew why Kerrie was remaining silent. It was her way of protecting Lori's feelings. These two women still cared for each other, and if Rudolph dropped off the face of the earth, Farrah had a feeling there would be no need for her services here today.

But Rudolph was alive and well and sitting across from her being a total jerk. Was greed the only factor motivating him? Farrah thought. Little did he know Farrah would be successful with this case because, whether they realized it or not, the two women's friendship had always been solid as a rock. Now it was time for Farrah to remind them of that.

"So tell me, Ms. Byers. When did your friendship with Ms. Shaw begin?" Though the woman seemed surprised, Farrah knew why she'd asked the question. She intended to make them recall why they'd become friends in the first place, in hopes they'd realize their relationship was too important to give up.

Lori glanced over at Kerrie and smiled as if remembering. "It was my first year of high school. I was thirteen and the new kid in town since my parents had moved to the city over the summer. Kerrie lived on my block and invited me to walk home with her. We became best friends immediately, and—"

"Why are we rehashing all of that stuff?" Rudolph said in a snarl. "We need to be discussing the money and—"

"Rudolph, if you're not happy with the way things are going here, you can leave!" Lori spoke up and said to her husband. It was apparent the man was surprised by his wife's sharp statement, and like a spoiled child, he pushed his chair back and stormed from the room, slamming the door behind him

Farrah waited a beat to see if Lori would run after him. Instead, the woman seemed to remain calm, and then after a few moments she continued the story of how she and Kerrie had met.

Farrah fought to hide her smile. Now she felt they would finally get somewhere.

Xavier glanced at his watch. It was close to three in the afternoon, and he hadn't received a response yet from the text message he'd sent to Farrah earlier inviting her to a Broadway play tonight. He had decided against calling her since he hadn't known the hours she would be tied up with the case she was mediating.

When his cell phone rang, he quickly picked it up and smiled when he saw the caller was Farrah. "Yes?"

"Xavier, it's Farrah. Sorry I didn't have time to text you back earlier, but I was in mediation sessions all day."

"How did it go?"

"Rather well, actually. At least it did once the husband left. He was determined to cause problems. I spent most of the day reminding the two women why they became friends in the first place. I think another session will resolve things. That is if the wife doesn't go home and let her husband's manipulations undo all we've achieved today. He seems to have a lot of influence on her."

Xavier nodded. "Are you still at work?"

"No, I just got back to the hotel and am about to take a long, leisurely bubble bath. I'm running the water as hot as I can stand it to unfreeze my bones. It's still extremely cold outside."

Xavier paused a moment and then asked, "Have you given any thought to joining me tonight for a Broadway play? The one I thought you'd enjoy is *Hair.* And I promise to keep you warm again if you do venture out."

That's what I'm afraid of, Farrah thought, sitting on the edge of her bed. The only reason she hadn't swooned each and every time she'd thought of the kiss they'd shared in the car last night was because it had taken all of her time and energy getting Kerrie and Lori to stroll back down memory lane.

"Umm, I've always wanted to see *Hair*," she said softly.

"Here's your chance."

Yes, here was her chance. Should she take it or should she let the opportunity drift in the wind because she didn't trust herself around one particular man? Would he try kissing her again? She drew in a deep breath knowing he would and knowing she would be disappointed if he didn't.

She had gone to bed last night with that hot and sizzling kiss on her mind and too many warm, touchy-feely emotions stirring in her heart. And she knew why. During the year she and Xavier had been bed partners, he'd had a way of making her feel special and had taken whatever time was needed to bring her as much pleasure as any one woman could possibly handle. He had been more attentive to her in that one year than Dustin had been during the four years of their marriage. She had missed Xavier's attentiveness, his presence, his lovemaking and every single thing about him.

Now he was back, not in her life on a routine basis but just for the period of time she would be here in New York. When they returned to Charlotte, things would go back to normal, with him having his life and her having hers. Their paths would rarely cross, and on those occasions when they might run into each other, she was satisfied they'd know they could never become lovers again.

Sharing a kiss wasn't so bad, and the way he'd given attention to her breasts wasn't a sin and a shame either. But she couldn't share a bed with him. That would be her ultimate downfall. If he ever went inside her body again she would be tempted to never, ever let him out. She could possibly get hooked back on what it had taken six months to wean herself from.

Could she handle his presence, his closeness and his heat without temptation pushing her on her back with him on top of her? She nibbled on her bottom lip while thinking, yes, she would handle it, even if it almost killed her. All she would have to do was close her eyes and see Dustin's face to remember why such a thing was necessary.

"Farrah?"

She drew in a deep breath. "Yes, I'd love to go see *Hair* with you. What time does the show begin?"

"Eight. I'll be there to pick you up around seven if that's okay with you."

"That's fine. I'll be waiting for you in the lobby."

She hung up the phone knowing she needed to build up her resolve that no matter what, she would not be sharing a bed with Xavier while she was in New York.

Chapter 6

"Circle around the block a few times, Jules. I should be back out in a few minutes."

"Yes, Mr. Kane."

Xavier tightened the coat around him as he made his way toward the hotel's entrance. He was early, intentionally so, and that meant Farrah would not be in the lobby waiting on him, ready to go. He would let her know he'd arrived and ask if he could come up to her hotel room.

He was a man who usually didn't like playing games; however, under these circumstances, he wasn't averse to having a game plan. He couldn't help but smile when he thought of all the things Cameron had done to win Vanessa over. For Xavier, it wasn't that kind of party, definitely not one that serious. All he wanted was his bed partner back, not a woman to make his wife. So he wouldn't go to the extremes as Cam had done.

However, he knew the key to winning a woman over was to discover her weakness and use it against her. He had no problem doing that if it meant getting his libido back on track. He needed to use the same tactic Farrah had mentioned she'd used on the two women with whom she was holding mediation sessions. He would force Farrah to remember what they once had and why it was way too good to give up.

He glanced around the lobby before pulling out his cell phone. He swiped his finger across Farrah's name that was already programmed in his iPhone. She picked up immediately. "Yes?"

"I arrived a little early. If you're not ready I can come up and wait."

"No need. I'm ready."

He was surprised. "You are?"

"Yes," she said, and he could swear he heard a smile in her voice. "For some reason I figured you might be early."

He lifted a brow. "Did you?"

"Yes."

He didn't like the sound of that. Was she on to him and his game plan? Hell, he hoped not. "Well, I'm here."

"And I'll be right down, Xavier."

She clicked off the phone, and Xavier was about to return the phone to his pocket when it rang. He hoped it was Farrah saying she'd changed her mind, and he could come up to her room anyway. Instead, it was York.

"Yes, Y?"

"What are you doing tonight? How about coming over for a beer and to shoot some pool?"

York, a former officer for the NYPD who now owned his own security firm in Queens, loved to play pool and was pretty damn good at it. There was a time he used to participate in tournaments around the country.

"Sorry, I have a date."

He could hear York's chuckle. "Hell, you don't go out on dates, X. All you do is make booty calls. That's been your M.O. for years."

Xavier frowned. Had it? Come to think of it, yes, it had been. After Dionne, he'd made sure no other woman got close to his heart, although they'd been more than welcome to share a bed with him, preferably theirs. What he would do was select a woman, get to know her well enough to suit him and then begin showing up at her place with a bottle of wine determined to get just one thing. He'd operated that way with every woman he'd slept with.

Including Farrah.

Why did the thought of grouping Farrah with all his other bed partners leave a bad taste in his mouth? Probably for the same reason he'd stayed with her longer than the others. For him, eleven months was a long time to sleep with the same woman. Hell, normally something like that could get downright boring. But there hadn't been a damn boring thing about Farrah. She had made her bed one of the most exciting places to be. But, like the others, he'd never invited her over to his place to share his bed. Umm, he would have to remedy that one day.

"So, who is she, X?"

He couldn't very well say she wasn't someone York knew since Xavier had introduced Farrah to all five of his godbrothers at Donovan and Natalie's wedding in June. But what he could do was be evasive as hell, which wouldn't be the first time. "Why do you want to know? And aren't you supposed to be checking out Ellie's friend Darcy?"

He smiled as he could actually hear York growling through the cell phone. "Hell, don't mess with me like that, X. The woman and I don't get along. I'm convinced she hates my guts."

Xavier laughed. Bad blood had developed between the two when, during Darcy's first week of moving to New York, she'd encountered a burglar who'd broken into her home while she slept. By the time the police had arrived, Darcy Owens had already administered her own brand of punishment to the unsuspecting criminal, who hadn't known she had a black belt in karate.

Ellie had gotten York out of bed to go across town to check on her friend. When he'd gotten there and discovered what had happened, he'd raked Darcy over the coals for placing her life in danger instead of letting the NYPD handle it. Darcy evidently hadn't appreciated York's attitude, and the two hadn't been exactly bosom buddies since. Frankly, Xavier had a feeling York liked Darcy more than he was letting on.

"You still haven't told me who's your date, X."

At that moment the bell over the elevator sounded, the door opened and Farrah walked out. Xavier smiled. *Saved by the bell.* "And I won't. Goodbye, Y."

He quickly disconnected the call and stuffed the phone in his coat pocket. His smile widened when Farrah came to a stop in front of him. She was wearing her full-length coat again, but he couldn't wait to see the outfit she had on underneath it. "Ready?"

She smiled up at him. "Yes, I'm ready."

Xavier doubted very seriously that Farrah Langley was ready for what he had in store for her tonight.

"The play was wonderful, Xavier. Thanks for taking me," Farrah said, glancing across the length of the rear car seat. She really hadn't been surprised when he'd swept her off her feet again to put her in the car at the hotel, and again when they'd arrived and left the theater. But she was surprised he had kept distance between them in the car now.

Although he'd ordered the privacy shield drawn and the lights dimmed, things were a lot different tonight than they had been last night when she'd practically sat in his lap during the car ride back to the hotel, and he'd kissed her so fervently her panties got wet.

"I thought so, too," he agreed. "And I'm glad you enjoyed it."

She glanced out the window and saw they were

headed in the opposite direction from her hotel. "Where are we going?"

"I thought I'd take you for a ride across the river on a ferry boat."

"A ferry boat? In this weather?"

He chuckled. "It's a private barge and we won't have to get out of the car. I thought you'd like seeing the Statue of Liberty up close."

"You were able to arrange something like that tonight? At this hour?"

"Yes, as much as security would allow, which is understandable."

She nodded, knowing it was. She looked out the window and saw they were at the New York harbor. Several huge cruise ships were docked, and glass lanterns that were hanging from light fixtures brightened up the entire area.

"Everything is ready, Mr. Kane. Should we proceed?" the driver asked over the intercom.

"Yes, Jules, and you can darken the lights back here."

On cue, the lights in the panel of both doors went out, drenching the rear of the car in total blackness. The only illumination came from the light reflecting off the tall buildings of the Manhattan skyline.

Farrah knew the exact moment the car drove onto the huge barge, and moments later she heard the sound of the car door opening and closing. She glanced questioningly over at Xavier.

"Jules is leaving," he said. "He's joining the captain of the barge in the wheelhouse. They're old friends."

"Oh." She knew that meant that she and Xavier would be in the car alone.

Moments later she could actually feel the swish and sway of the water beneath them when the barge began moving. She had ridden a ferry once before while visiting a friend in Florida. It had been a passenger ferry, and it had been during daylight hours. However, this ferry ride provided a beautiful view of New York City at night.

She glanced over at Xavier. He was still sitting across from her and was looking at her. Although the lights reflected off his features, she couldn't see his entire face. However, knowing his eyes were on her was enough to send a luscious shiver up her spine.

Why did he have to be so mind-bogglingly handsome? Why did being here with him and sharing this space with him remind her of other times she'd shared more than space with him? She couldn't help but recall when she had shared her body, given it to him whenever and however he'd wanted it.

She decided the best thing to do was strike up a conversation to ease the heated tension flowing between them, although she doubted it would do a single thing to douse the hot-blooded desire flowing through her veins.

"We won't be running into the passenger ferry that runs twenty-four hours a day, will we?" she asked.

"No, we're taking a different route so we're safe."

She wondered just how safe she was alone with him in the darkened backseat of a car while rolling down the Hudson. There was the scent of a predatory male circulating in the air, but she was determined to stay in her corner. If anyone made the first move it would be him…although he didn't seem in a rush to do so.

Silence hovered between them for a few moments, and then he asked, "Would you like some wine, Farrah?"

She lifted a brow. "You have wine in here?"

"Yes."

He proceeded to press a button, and a compartment opened that transformed into a minibar.

"Wow, I'm impressed," she said.

He chuckled. "Are you?"

"Yes."

He uncorked the wine bottle and poured two glasses. He then leaned over and handed one to her. "Umm, you smell good," he said in a deep, throaty voice.

They were passing beneath a brightly lit building that illuminated his features. Heated lust was definitely shining in the dark depths of his eyes.

"Thanks. I think."

He smiled. "You aren't sure?"

She took a sip of her wine, liking how it tasted on her tongue. She looked at her wine in the glass and then at him. "Yes, I'm sure. I think you smell good, too. I guess our noses are in rare form tonight."

"That's not the only thing. Slide over here for a moment."

Farrah met his gaze and decided she was either a

glutton for punishment or eager for pleasure. Ignoring the voice inside her head advising her to stay put, she slid over the warm leather seat toward him. What she'd told him earlier was the truth. He smelled good. Good enough to lick all over.

When she was basically plastered to his side, he stretched his arm across the back of the seat. "Now," he said when she was snuggled close to him, "this is where you belong."

"Is it?"

"Yes."

She would have thought such a statement—a bold proclamation made by him or any man about where she belonged—was out of order and deserved a blistering retort, but she didn't have time to do so when he eased the glass from her hand and placed it in the holder next to his seat.

Then he turned toward her. "You have on too many clothes," he whispered in a deep, husky voice.

"Mainly to stay warm. I get cold easily," was her response.

"I promised to keep you warm, didn't I?"

"Yes, but that was last night."

He began unbuttoning her coat. "That promise stands whenever we're together."

Farrah drew in a deep breath as she studied his face. His gaze was focused on every button he was opening as if what he was doing was a very important task. She knew she should probably tell him that when it came to promises from men, she found they didn't hold water, so he didn't have to waste his time making one that he expected her to believe. But for some reason she couldn't say it. Not when he had kept her warm last night. And not when he was taking his time now, handling her like she was a piece of fine china. He was opening each button slowly, with painstaking deliberateness, as if he was about to expose something beneath her coat other than the short blue dress she was wearing.

The dress might be short, true enough, but her black leather boots were long, stopping at her knees. Did he intend to remove them as well? Would she let him? Before she could think further on that question, he whispered, "Now scoot up a bit so I can work your arms out of the sleeves."

Like a dutiful child, she did what she was told. When she leaned forward, she placed her hand on his thigh and almost snatched it back when she felt his hard erection. Her eyes flew to his face and there was nothing apologetic about the look staring back at her. Instead it was a look that almost made her regret they were no longer bed partners.

And she didn't want to have any regrets. Although she'd found it extremely difficult to forget him and get beyond everything they'd shared, she was convinced she had done the right thing when she'd made up in her mind not to fall back in bed with him.

Fate, it seemed, was working against her now. It was as if some fragment of her brain was trying to convince her that getting back with him would be a fantasy come true and that her sex-deprived body would thank her for the chance to get laid again. But a part of her, the part that had endured pain of the worst kind at the hands of a man she'd once loved, was holding back, keeping that guardrail around her heart firmly in place. She doubted that even Xavier could knock it down.

She knew she should remove her hand from his thigh, but the feel of his erection beneath her palm was doing something to her, reminding her how it had been a vital part of her life at one time. And how it had given her so much pleasure.

She felt his erection begin to throb beneath her fingertips, a slow, steady pulsating thump that was causing her hand to tremble while causing certain parts of her body to vibrate. She was so in tune to this part of him and remembered well how once it was inside of her, it could stroke her into a frenzy of the sweetest kind. She felt the inner muscles of her feminine core clench just thinking about it.

Farrah glanced up and met his gaze when he pushed the coat off her shoulders. There was a look in his eyes that sent a delicious warmth through her body. She couldn't help wondering how she had endured a half year without this. Without him.

When her coat was off, he tossed it to the other side of the backseat and his gaze slid down the length of her outfit, which wasn't much. What little it was seemed to have his attention.

"I like blue," he said, running his fingers along the hem of her dress.

"Do you?"

"Yes. It's my favorite color. And these boots look good on you."

She smiled. "Thanks."

"So tell me," he said, easing closer to her after removing his own coat and lowering his head to whisper huskily in her ear. "What does a man like me have to do to get you out of a dress like this?"

She grinned and looked at him. "Umm, I don't know, Mr. Kane. You've always seemed to be a very innovative kind of guy. What do you have in mind?"

She couldn't help but take note that her hand was still on his thigh, still in contact with his throbbing erection. For some reason she couldn't let go just yet.

"What I have in mind is stripping you out of every stitch of clothing you have on. Here and now. What do you think about that?"

She couldn't help but chuckle. "Umm, not sure that's a good idea."

"But you would consider it?"

She smiled upon seeing the challenging glean in his eyes. "Let's just say I don't have a problem with you trying to convince me that I should consider it."

He didn't say anything for a minute, as if giving her words some thought. "I hope you know I can be very convincing when I want to be."

"I'm very much aware of that."

She knew Xavier well enough to understand her words were like a carrot dangling in his face. A carrot he intended to devour. This was the most fun she'd had lately. The summer months had been a complete bore to her and autumn hadn't been much better. When Natalie and Donovan had returned from their honeymoon, the amorous newlyweds hadn't socialized a lot, preferring to stay inside behind closed doors, probably burning the sheets. So with no lover to sleep with, no best friend to talk to, Farrah had had a lot of free time on her hands and had wondered if she'd done the right thing in breaking things off with Xavier.

But then, all it had taken was running into Dustin, his wife and daughter at the mall one Sunday evening in mid-October to recall why it had been the only thing she could do in order to protect herself and not get hurt by any man again.

"So what do you think about the view?"

She looked past Xavier to glance out the window. It was hard to believe they were in a car, riding down the Hudson on a barge. If he had deliberately set out to impress her, he had achieved that goal. "The view is beautiful. You definitely know how to wow a girl. I'm impressed."

"Are you?"

"Yes."

"Enough to let me take this dress off you?"

She shook her head smiling. "You won't give up, will you?"

"Not until I have you naked."

There was a determination in his tone that made shivers run up and down her spine. Heat began spreading through her stomach, and she felt a tingling sensation take life between her legs. She wondered if he had any idea just what was happening to her, how much she was fighting the temptation of giving him everything he was asking for. And then some.

She looked past him out the window again. Only Xavier would go to this trouble to impress a woman. And it was working.

Farrah glanced back at him, and the look he was giving her sent a burst of desire exploding through her. She found herself leaning toward him and his masculine mouth that was so sexy it should be declared illegal.

"And once you have me naked, what's next?"

The erection beneath her hand seemed to get larger. "Then I plan to taste you all over."

With his words, blatant and hot, her thighs seem to automatically spread apart, and she couldn't help but remember how it felt to have his tongue between them, licking her with hungry strokes to sweet oblivion, fueling not one orgasm but several.

"So what do you think of that, Farrah?"

She swallowed, not wanting to think at all. Her body was pushing her to feel instead. Making her crave things she was better off not having, but making those damn hot memories invade her mind anyway. They were just too delicious to ignore.

She met his gaze, felt the heat emanating from the dark depths. And it was heat that was generating a slow yet intense sizzle within her. "Why are you doing this to me, Xavier?"

Without responding, his gaze seemed to say it all. The heat from his eyes nearly burned off her remaining clothes. Lust flowed up her spine as a fierce degree of need filled her all over. He continued to look at her, saying nothing, yet saying everything.

"I think you know the answer to that, Farrah," he finally said in a deep, throaty voice. "But in case there's a possibility that you don't, the reason is simple. I never got over you. Our split was your idea, not mine."

She lifted a brow. "But you didn't disagree."

"Because I knew it was what you wanted."

"And now?"

"And now I plan to convince you that decision was a mistake."

She saw the determination in his gaze. "What if I said you can't do that?"

A smile touched his lips. "Then I would say I intend to die trying. I want you back, Farrah."

Farrah knew he was dead serious. She forced herself to breathe in before asking, "And you think wanting me back is simple?"

A smile touched the corners of his lips. "Yes, wanting you back is simple, but *getting* you back will be the hard part." He paused and then said, "And speaking of hard…"

She held his gaze as the throb beneath her hand increased, and she could feel his erection grow and harden even more. "Yes, what about it?" she asked, not even trying to ignore the burning sensation in the pit of her stomach.

He placed his hand over hers. "For the past six months, I've been working hard, Farrah, harder than

I wanted to. But I had to do it as a way to try to forget you. And I failed at doing that."

She nibbled on her bottom lip, surprised that Xavier would admit something like that. It would have been just as easy, less messy and a whole lot simpler for her to think he had moved on without any passing thoughts of her and what they'd shared. But to know he had thought of her, had worked doubly hard to forget her, yet failed, made something inside her swell to gigantic proportions, and that wasn't good.

"And can you honestly say you didn't think of me, Farrah?" he then asked.

That question was a no-brainer. Of course she had thought about him. Constantly. Every day. In the middle of the night. When she woke up in the morning. And she'd definitely thought of him during those times her body went through a physical meltdown when it needed the kind of toss between the sheets only he could give her.

She could admit such a thing now, while sitting here with him alone, in the privacy of a car where they had a spacious backseat. She had no qualms saying it because regardless of all of that, she believed she had done the right thing in ending their affair.

And she would be doing the right thing in not letting him talk her into starting things back up again between them.

"Yes, I thought about you, Xavier, but I *had* to end things between us for all the right reasons," she said quietly.

"And what are these right reasons?"

Now that would be a little harder to explain. How could she eloquently break it down so he would understand that she had to end things to keep her sanity? That with him, for the first time since breaking up with Dustin, she had begun to feel things, want things and need things that she knew could only cause her heartbreak.

How could she explain to him that every time he showed up at her place, looked at her, touched her, tasted her and made love to her until she screamed her throat raw, her heart swelled? That was the part she wouldn't try explaining since there were some things about a woman's emotions that a man didn't need to know or understand.

She had gotten a lot smarter since her Dustin days, but because of Xavier, the part of her heart that had hardened had begun to soften each time she saw him, each time he held her in his arms and kissed her with that sinful tongue of his.

"Tell me, Farrah."

Gathering her control, she removed her hand from his thigh and shifted in her seat, placing her hand into her own lap. For this she needed some semblance of detachment and distance…as much as she could get. But she was well aware that no matter how much space she put between them, she would still be able to feel his heat, the same heat that could succeed in melting the ice encasing her heart. But he needed to hear what she had to say.

"You know my history with Dustin."

He nodded. "Yes."

She drew in a deep breath. Discussing her ex-husband had never been on the agenda. But one night when Xavier had come over she'd been caught in one of her melancholy moods. She had run into Dustin earlier that day in a department store, and he'd tried of all things to flirt with her. The bastard who'd left her for another woman had actually tried coming on to her, tried to entice her to leave the department store and have an evening of sex with him in a hotel across the street. He'd said his wife would never find out and that they would be doing it for old times' sake.

Dustin had claimed his problem with her had never been in the bedroom, but said her constant travels for her job were to blame for the loneliness that had forced him to seek out other women. He had actually tried to make her feel responsible for his adulterous behavior.

Any other woman probably would have fallen for his pitiful spiel, but she had stopped being Dustin's fool the day he'd asked her for a divorce. She doubted she would ever forgive him for the hurt and humiliation that he'd caused her.

"I don't ever want to go through anything like that again," she heard herself saying.

Xavier's mouth drew in a tight line. "I can respect that, but what does that have to do with me?"

"A good question," she murmured softly to herself. He probably didn't see the connection because, for him, there truly wasn't one. Nothing about his purpose in seeking her out then and now had changed. He was footloose and fancy-free and intended to stay that way. He shied away from serious relationships, preferring to make his booty calls whenever, wherever and to whomever he desired with no strings attached. He was a man, and he could go through that type of program without any emotional attachments. She'd tried the same but found that she just couldn't do it. Especially with Xavier.

"What it has to do with you, Xavier, is that I felt the time had come for me to take a step back from our little affair. Eleven months was way too long for me. We were getting too complacent."

She wanted to express herself in a way where she didn't come off sounding like a needy woman. God knows she didn't want that. Since her divorce she had tried not to depend on anyone—especially a man—for her happiness. But with Xavier she had found herself slipping.

When he didn't say anything, she continued. "That first night you came over we agreed to have a no-strings-attached affair, and I felt we had run our course."

He nodded. "Have there been any men since me, Farrah?"

His question surprised her. It would be so easy to say it wasn't any of his business and let him assume there had been others. After all, he'd probably slept with other women since her. Something kept the lie from forming on her lips, however. Instead she said, "No, I've been too busy." That really wasn't a total lie.

"And I haven't had another woman since you," he said in a throaty tone.

His words shocked her; in fact, they left her speechless. He hadn't had another woman since her? Xavier, the man with a sex drive that never quit? At that moment she couldn't explain the satisfied pleasure she felt blooming inside of her. Why had he denied himself?

"Seems like we have the same problem, Farrah."

She pulled herself back into the conversation, trying to tread lightly while all kinds of wicked thoughts flowed through her. "And what problem is that?"

He reached out and rubbed his thumb over her bottom lip. "We need to get unleashed. You need a man to make love to you like I need to make love to a woman. Bad. But I don't need to make love to any woman, Farrah. I need to make love to you. I so miss hearing you scream."

More sensations washed over her, wetting her panties, causing every nerve ending in her body to respond to the sensuality in his voice and the heat in his words. She had definitely missed him making her scream as well.

"So you think we need to get unleashed, huh?" she asked in a low tone, while her heartbeat throbbed in her chest.

"Yes, but due to schedule restraints, I'll just have time to prime you for now."

Oh, she knew all about his priming methods and just what setting up for that stage of seduction could do to her. They'd never made out in a car before, and just the thought of doing so was downright naughty. But she felt like being naughty tonight. She had been a good girl for a long time and felt the need to sexually unwind. But more than anything, she wanted to scream. She shuddered at the thought of all he was offering her on a sensual platter.

"So what do you think about that plan, Farrah?"

At the moment she didn't want to think. She didn't want to talk.

Instead she leaned close to him, deciding she needed to respond to him this way. She intended to start off by initiating a game they'd often played when he'd come over to her place. She leaned close and offered him the tip of her tongue. Just as expected, he swooped down quickly and all but sucked her tongue into his mouth.

She moaned deep in her throat as familiar sensations burned in her soul. The strength of the passion he was evoking within her was the same as it had been from the first. Xavier could make a woman want things she was better off not having.

As she proceeded to melt under the force of his kiss, she knew that somehow she would take whatever he was offering for now and then find the strength to walk away and not look back when their time together in New York ended.

Chapter 7

Xavier knew the moment Farrah surrendered.

He was practically on his back with her draped all over him while she took his mouth with a hunger that he was more than willing to reciprocate.

God, he wanted her with a vengeance. It wouldn't take much to zip down his pants, pull out his shaft and ease right into her. She had made it easy to do so with the way her thighs were positioned over his. He remembered—not that he could ever forget—that she preferred wearing skimpy panties, thongs or the barely-there kind. He'd bet nothing had changed in that area. Hell, he was hoping as much.

She pulled back, breaking off the kiss, and he drew in a deep breath as he gazed up into her face. She was the spitting image of a woman unleashed, a woman

who knew what she wanted and planned on getting it.
A woman who had gone long enough without a lover.
He intended to change that. Right here. Right now.

He drew in a deep breath and swallowed hard when,
not bothering to unbuckle his belt, she jerked his shirt
from the waistband of his pants before proceeding to
ease down his zipper. He didn't have to ask what she was
about to do; he just hoped he would be able to survive
the experience.

When she smiled at him while licking her lips, his
heart began beating frantically in his chest. She had
effectively turned the tables on him. He was supposed
to be seducing her and not the other way around. What
about that control he was known for? Hell, it was slipping, and there was nothing he could do about it now.
At the moment he couldn't deny her anything, especially
the piece of him she obviously wanted.

And when he felt her warm fingers probing inside
his pants, anticipation sizzled up his spine, and it took
all he could do not to moan out loud. After she pulled
his erection free, he watched through lowered lashes as
she studied his shaft, as if she was savoring the thought
of tasting him and trying to decide the best way to go
about it.

Then her fingers started moving as she began to
stroke it, palmed him in her hand, pumped him with her
fingers. His body shuddered, and heat surged through
him, especially in his groin.

She glanced up at him and smiled as his belly
clenched with the look he saw in her eyes. The fire he

saw there not only sharpened his senses but had his erection expanding right in her hands.

"I'm about to show you, Xavier Kane, that you're not the only one who knows about priming. And don't you dare think about pulling my mouth away until I'm ready to let go."

She didn't give him a chance to think, let alone respond, when her mouth lowered and took him in.

"Heaven help me." He murmured the words in a heated rush of breath, closed his eyes and released a deep, guttural groan.

Her mouth seemed to expand to encompass his erection all the way from the head to the root, and when she began using her tongue in full earnest, pleasure—which he hadn't felt in six months—shot through every part of his body.

With slow thoroughness, she took her time torturing him, letting him see that she was the one in control of this, and when her mouth deliberately began exerting pressure to the head of his erection, he clenched his jaw, and his body rumbled into one hell of an explosion.

When he gripped the side of her head and tried pulling her away, she planted her teeth on him with enough pressure to remind him of her earlier order. She was in control.

When his turn came, she was going to be sorry, he thought as his jaw clenched tight and the climax shook him. He wondered if he was still breathing. Surely he had died, gotten buried and gone to heaven.

Then before he could recover from that first explosion, another one hit; this one even stronger, and he felt all kinds of sensations tear up the length of his body and back.

"Farrah!"

If he thought she was ready to let go, then evidently he was out of his mind. The latter was true anyway. He was definitely out of his mind with all the scintillating excitement thrown in the mix. And he saw that she was determined not to release him until the last shudder eased from his body.

It was then that he slowly forced open his eyes and stared at her. It took every ounce of energy he possessed to reach out his hand to caress her cheek. He wasn't sure if he was imagining things or not, but her entire face took on an ethereal beauty that was more vibrant, more soul-touchingly exquisite than ever before.

And when she tilted her lips in a smile, he dragged in a staggering breath and felt his body getting hard all over again as desire once again enflamed him, filled him to capacity. But something else happened at that moment, too. He wasn't sure just what it was, since it was something he couldn't put a name to at that moment. But he was convinced it was something he'd never felt before, and he suddenly felt totally consumed by it.

"So what do you think, Xavier?"

Instead of answering, he moved quickly, and, ignoring her shriek of surprise, he eased her back and loomed over her. He caught her chin in his hand as his mouth came down on hers, effectively absorbing whatever words she was about to say. He intended to show her just what he thought.

* * *

His kiss tried taking control of her mouth, but Farrah refused to let it. She enjoyed sharing his heat, participating in such a sensual duel as their tongues tangled. Electricity flowed through her body.

And she still wanted more.

She intended to get it, and it seemed he was just as determined to give it to her. Okay, she could handle this, she thought. Then she wasn't all that sure when she felt his hands under her dress. When he finally released her mouth, she was breathless, left in a state of pure enthrallment. Totally awestruck. Mesmerized.

"You should never have pushed me over the edge, Farrah."

She met his gaze. Had she actually done that?

"You do know what that means, don't you?"

She nodded. Yes, she knew exactly what that meant. She'd had him in her mouth, and now he intended to have her in his. He didn't waste time pushing her dress up and out of his way before pulling her barely-there panties down past her thighs.

"Xavier, don't we need to talk about this?"

"No."

And that was the last word he said before lifting her hips with his hand and lowering his head between her legs. The moment the tip of his tongue eased between her feminine folds, she cried out, closed her eyes and reached out to grab hold of his shoulders.

How had she gone without this for so long? How had she survived without the feel of his mouth on her, in her, his tongue lapping her up before delving deeper and deeper. He was feasting on her, pushing her legs apart to treat himself to more of her.

A soft moan flowed from her lips. Then another. Pleasure began rolling over her in melodious waves, pushing her over the edge while at the same time taking her under. No inner part of her was left untouched. If his tongue could reach it, it was stroked. Mercilessly so.

Farrah suddenly cried out when she couldn't take any more, and rapture struck every inch of her body. He continued to devour her, as she quivered from an orgasm that would have topped the Richter scale. When he pulled back and captured her mouth, his tongue was still hot and hungry.

And she knew he wasn't through with her yet when she heard him tear open a condom package.

Then there it was. The head of his erection probing where his mouth had been. He lifted her hips up in his hands the moment he thrust into her. The surge of pleasure that ripped through her with this coming together made her scream. That only pushed him to go deeper, made his strokes stronger.

"Xavier!"

He lifted his head to stare down at her, and the primal look in his eyes almost made her lose her breath while at the same time it triggered another explosion within her. She had wanted to be naughty, but he was making her crazy.

And then he bucked, thrust harder, went deeper and her boot-clad legs tightened around him, greedy for everything he wanted to give and ready to take it. She didn't have long to wait for his release. Hot molten liquid shot everywhere inside of her, lubricating her inner walls with the very essence of him.

"Farrah!"

He had thrown his head back and her name came out as a deep growl from his throat, and he then lowered his head to take her mouth, to feed greedily off of it, as his body continued to thrust insatiably inside of her. Harder.

She screamed again as spasms shook her. When had making love to any man been this good? And she knew at that moment it could only be this way with Xavier.

He broke off the kiss, and his forehead came to rest against hers when their bodies slowed. She breathed in a deep, trembling breath as she stared up at him.

"Satisfied?" he asked, staring down at her. His shirt was unbuttoned to his waist and he was still wearing his pants. She could just imagine how erotic things would have gotten if they'd been naked.

"Very," she said, smiling up at him and meaning every word. He was still inside of her. Still hard. The man had more staying power than anyone she knew.

"Good." He paused a minute then asked, "So what do *you* think, Farrah?" It took her a moment to follow him. He was deliberately countering the question she'd asked him earlier.

She released a deep breath. "I can't think at the moment. Ask me again later."

He chuckled as he slowly eased out of her and

proceeded to pull her panties back up and pull her dress down. He then buttoned his shirt.

"I can just imagine what your driver is probably thinking, though," she said, sitting up.

Xavier chuckled. "Jules is probably grateful he got to spend time with his old Navy buddy. He's worked for me for a while and knows— "

"How you operate?"

He glanced over at her while tucking his shirt back inside his pants. For some reason, that statement bothered him. "And how do you think I operate, Farrah?"

She leaned back against the seat of the car and closed her eyes. "Ask me later. I told you, I can't think now. I just want to savor the moment."

And he thought he wouldn't mind savoring some more of her. Not understanding why he needed to do so, what exactly was driving him, he caught her off guard when he leaned over and kissed her with the same degree of passion he'd demonstrated earlier but with far less desperation. He wanted this to be slow pleasure that was meant to be savored, relished and enjoyed. And from the unhurried and leisurely way her tongue was mating with his, he knew that it was.

When he released her mouth, her head fell back against the seat cushions, and she stared at him as if she was incapable of saying anything. He couldn't help but smile, pleased he'd kissed any words from her lips for the time being.

"What was that for?" she finally was able to ask.

"Ask me later. I can't think now," he said rezipping his pants.

She laughed and playfully punched him in the arm. "Funny. You're a regular comedian who happens to be a damn good kisser."

"Earned brownie points, did I?"

"Yes, you most certainly did. I don't know many guys like you."

"I'm glad to hear it," he said, pulling his cell phone out of the pocket of his jacket and punching a lone number. "Jules, how far are we from port?" he asked, glancing out the window while working his arms into the sleeves of his jacket. He nodded and then said, "Good."

He clicked off the phone and replaced it in his jacket and glanced over at Farrah. "When we get back to your hotel, do I get invited up for a nightcap?"

"After what we did just now do you really think you need an invitation? Better yet, do you have the energy for more?"

He couldn't help but smile at that.

She frowned at him. "Forget I asked. Silly me. How could I forget your endless amount of energy? You know, this was the first time we did it some place other than my house," she said, reaching for her purse. He watched her pull out her makeup compact.

"First time for everything. I plan for us to start being adventurous," he said, working his tie back around his neck.

She clicked the compact closed and glanced over

at him. Surprise lit her eyes. "You do understand that nothing between us has changed."

Something fluttered in his chest. "What do you mean?" he asked.

She shrugged as if she assumed they were in one accord with what she was about to say. "Going back to our conversation earlier about restarting our affair… Spending time with you like this, here in New York, is wonderful, but when we return to Charlotte we won't be seeing each other again."

The hell we won't! He fought to keep the frown off his face while wondering just how she figured that. "I don't see why not. You've missed me. I've missed you. So there."

"Yes, which is the reason we're spending time together now. A holiday fling is just what we evidently need. It's the season to be jolly, and we can even act a little loony, out of character, even behave like sex addicts and all that good stuff. We're adults with needs. But when it's all said and done, eventually things have to get back to normal, and when they do, it will be life as we know it."

"And what kind of life is that?" he asked, trying to keep anger from burning the back of his throat.

"I can't speak for you, but mine will be one with no serious entanglements. I have too much baggage for any man to deal with."

Try me. He decided now was not the time to tell her that their entanglement was already as serious as it could get. He also decided not to break the news that he had all intentions of resuming what they had shared before. The only kind of life he planned on having was one with her in it.

He opened his mouth to speak but closed it when he heard them docking back at the port. A short time later the car door opened, and he knew Jules had returned. That gave him a chance to sit and ponder why he had this burning obsession with getting back with her. And he knew the reason had nothing to do with the off-the-chain sex they'd had tonight or all those other times before. It was way too deep for him to try and dissect at this moment. Especially when she thought she'd delivered the last word.

He fully understood why she intended to keep him at arm's length again once they returned to Charlotte. She'd been burned once and didn't intend for any man to light a match to her again. Well, he had news for her. He was not going to let her lump him in with that poor excuse for a husband any longer.

"You've gotten quiet on me, Xavier."

They were back on the road again. Bright lights were everywhere as the car headed back toward her hotel. "I was just thinking."

"About what?"

"What I need to do to convince you that we need to restart our affair on a long-term basis."

She shook her head. "Don't bother. I don't do long-term."

"You did me for one month shy of a year."

"I got carried away," she said simply. "*We* got carried

away. It was an abnormality for you as much as it was for me."

Yes, it had been, but he hadn't complained.

"And what about your status in the club?"

The question annoyed him. "Forget about the club."

"Why should I? And can you? You and your god-brothers are the ones who established it. What will they think?"

At the moment he didn't give a royal damn.

What had he been thinking when he'd conceived of the Bachelors in Demand Club, he wondered now. And at the time, his five godbrothers, for various reasons, had been more than happy to be a part of it.

"Xavier?"

He glanced over at her. "I'm still thinking."

She smiled. "Yes, you do that and pretty soon you'll see I'm right. What you're asking for is not what you really want. You just got caught up in the moment. You even admitted yourself that because of work you hadn't slept with another woman since me. The way I see it, you've been suffering from a bad case of horniness. Don't get your heads mixed up, Xavier. You used to be pretty good knowing one from the other."

He looked away out the window. She sounded like she assumed she had all the answers. Well, he had news for her. If she thought—

"And I think considering everything, we should forget about that nightcap."

At her interruption, he looked at her. "Are you saying you don't want me to spend the night with you?"

"I don't recall issuing you an invitation."

He frowned. "Are we into playing games now, Farrah?"

"No." She didn't say anything for a moment and then, "Look, Xavier, I'll spend every moment that I can with you while we're here in New York. I really want that. There's nothing wrong with enjoying the fun while it lasts."

There was a momentary pause, and then he asked, "But when we return to Charlotte, I can't call you or drop by like before?"

"I prefer that you didn't."

Did she really mean that, he asked himself. She was returning his stare with a straight face, and her tone of voice sounded serious enough. But still…

She was the same woman who'd come apart in his arms moments ago. The same woman who'd admitted to missing him, to trying to forget him these past six months.

He studied her features and saw the determined look in her eyes. However, he took a minute to look beyond that, and he could swear he saw something else. Was she really that scared to admit that possibly those eleven months they'd been together had meant more than just sex?

His eyebrows knit in a tight frown. This was getting pretty damn confusing. He should be in agreement with how she was thinking. She definitely expected him to be, but he just wasn't feeling it, and he needed a reality check to figure out why.

"Let's do dinner tomorrow night," he heard himself suggesting.

"That's fine, if I'm in town."

He lifted a brow. "Where will you be if not here?"

"Heading back to Charlotte if I wrap things up with my clients tomorrow. Either way I hope to be leaving by Friday."

A sense of dread felt like a sword twisting in his chest. Friday was two days away. "I want to spend time with you again before you leave, Farrah, and I agree tonight might not be a good time."

"I'll call you tomorrow, Xavier. That's the best I can do."

She was deliberately giving him little to work with, but she didn't know that Xavier worked best under pressure. He would take tonight to go home and regroup, plan a new strategy and decide just what he intended to do about Farrah Langley.

One thing was for certain. He had no intentions of letting her go. If she thought things were over between them, then she definitely had another thought coming.

Chapter 8

Farrah wrapped the huge towel around her as she stepped out of the shower. From where she stood in the bathroom she could see her bed, and if anyone would have told her she would be sleeping in it alone tonight, without Xavier, she would not have believed them.

There was no reason for him not to have spent the night…at least there hadn't been a reason until he began spouting all that nonsense about them continuing their affair once they returned to Charlotte. What could he have been thinking to even suggest such a thing?

As she slipped into her nightgown, she shook her head, totally confused. Tonight had been an adventure, definitely something new and different. She smiled, thinking she liked the idea of being naughty. She liked the idea of a holiday affair, too.

A casual relationship was all she was interested in. With Xavier, however, what had started out as a strictly no-strings affair had slipped into a hot and heavy routine, a full-blown sexual habit they couldn't kick. Not that they'd tried. The more he'd shown up on her doorstep, the more she'd wanted him to keep coming.

And that wasn't good.

He could argue with her on that point all day long, and she would not change her mind and relent. As far as she was concerned, they either agreed to indulge in a New York affair or nothing.

Then why, she thought a short while later when she slipped between the sheets of her lonely bed, was she thinking of him and all they'd done that night? What they'd shared for eleven months, and more importantly, what she'd gone without the past six months and what she would continue to go without?

If tonight had been a calculated move on his part to stir up memories, then she would be the first to say he'd succeeded. As she lay staring up at the ceiling, she couldn't get out of her mind just how he'd felt inside of her, killing her softly with every sensual stroke.

So many memories began swirling around in her head, making sleep impossible. At least for now. Instead, she couldn't help but recall the first time he'd shown up on her doorstep and how quickly and easily she'd tumbled with him into her bed. She'd opened the door, and he'd stood there, wearing a pair of jeans and a white shirt and looking as sexy as any man had a right to look. There had been something about him that had wowed

her from the first time she'd seen him that night at the
Racetrack Café. She'd heard about him and the bachelor
club he was affiliated with, but until she'd seen him for
herself, she hadn't known how any man could have that
effect on a woman.

She'd known she had wanted him from the start,
passionately so, and hadn't intended to let something
like protocol stand in her way. She'd seen him as a way
to have fun and forget about all the hurt Dustin had
caused her. She'd wanted to know how it felt to have a
no-strings-attached affair and not care one iota if she
saw the man again. She'd wanted an affair that was as
casual as it could get.

And that's what she'd gotten in the beginning. But
then she'd noticed things beginning to change, even if he
hadn't. Probably because those changes had been one-
sided. There was no reason to assume that he'd begun
thinking about her in the wee hours of the night and
anticipating the next time they would hook up. Or find
himself smiling in the middle of the day after thinking
of something that happened between them the night
before. And she was pretty confident that when she did
open the door for him, he didn't feel that funny feeling
in the pit of his stomach.

Those had been the warning signs, and she'd had no
reason not to heed them and put in place any and every
preventive measure that she could. Nothing seemed to
work. The situation seemed to get worse. And she'd
known the best thing to do was to break things off with
him completely.

And now he wanted to jump-start things again and had done a pretty good job giving her a reason to do so. But she couldn't. Bottom line was that she was dealing with something he couldn't understand. It was only about sex for him, but for her she was taking every memory as seriously as it could get.

She moved to another position, not that she thought that would help. It would be a sleepless night. Even after the workout Xavier had given her tonight, her feminine core was achy, in need of some intimate attention, Xavier Kane style.

Give in to him, a voice inside her head whispered. *You're a big girl. You can handle another affair with Xavier. It would be up to you to make sure it's an affair that leads nowhere. And if it did, what's another little broken heart? What's the big deal?*

The big deal was there in his eyes each and every time he looked at her. It was there on his tongue every time he kissed her. It was embedded in the fingers that touched her.

After a few tosses and turns, she discovered she still couldn't get to sleep and decided she needed to talk to someone, and there was no other person she could share her woes with than her best friend.

She glanced over at the clock and cringed when she saw it was almost one o'clock. She didn't know what kind of hours Natalie was keeping now, but before she was married, Dr. Natalie Ford Steele, esteemed chemistry professor at Princeton University, used to be up at all hours of the night.

She grabbed her cell phone off the nightstand and punched in one number that automatically connected to Natalie. The phone was picked up on the first ring. "Hey, Farrah, what's going on?"

Farrah smiled, grateful to hear her friend's bubbly voice at a minute before one in the morning. "Evidently, you are. I take it you aren't sleep."

"Heavens, no. I just finished another chapter of this book I'm working on and was sitting here cuddled on the sofa enjoying a cup of hot chocolate."

She then remembered that Natalie was working on what would probably be another New York Times bestseller on global warming. "Where's Donovan?"

"Oh, he went to bed hours ago. I think the triplets wore him out. We kept them earlier while Cheyenne and Quade went shopping to play Santa. They are definitely three busy beavers. Donovan and I could barely keep up with them."

Farrah chuckled. "Are you two having second thoughts about having kids of your own now?"

"Never! I want Donovan's baby so bad."

Natalie's words made something twist in her heart when she remembered how she had wanted Dustin's baby, too. Instead of giving a child to her, he'd given one to someone else. That pain reminded her why she could never give her heart to another man.

"So what's up, Farrah?"

She swallowed. There was no reason to talk anything over with Natalie now. Not with the reminder she'd just gotten. The pain was still stabbing her chest. "Nothing."

"Um, I know you, girl. You would not have called me at one in the morning for nothing. Go on. Let it out. What's bothering you?"

Farrah nibbled on her bottom lip a minute before saying, "I ran into Xavier yesterday."

There was a pause on the other end, which Farrah understood. Natalie knew why she had broken things off with Xavier. "In that case, I'm sure cold New York is probably pretty hot by now."

Farrah threw her head back and laughed, especially when she remembered how hot things had gotten while riding across the Hudson in Xavier's private car. She then cleared her throat. "Hey, what can I say?"

"You can say the two of you have decided to get back together."

The smile on Farrah's face immediately became a frown. She'd known that Natalie liked Xavier. What was there not to like? Besides being good-looking as sin, he was also a downright nice person. She would attest to that. And of course he was one of Donovan's closest friends. But all of that had nothing to do with her heart.

"No, we're not getting back together, although he suggested such a thing. I told him I'd indulge in a holiday fling while we're here in New York. That was the best I could do."

Understandably there was another pause, which was

followed by a feminine snort. "I wish you would rethink that proposal, Farrah. Not all men are like Dustin."

Farrah changed positions in bed while she rolled her eyes. How many times had she heard that very thing—not only from Natalie, but from several others? "I don't want to try and weed the good from the bad. Casual affairs suit me just fine, but the one with Xavier was beginning to get too hot, heavy and addictive."

"That's not bad with the right guy, Farrah. Hey, let's run down a few things."

"A few things like what?"

"Why Xavier might be a keeper."

There was no doubt in Farrah's mind that he was a keeper. All she had to do was concentrate on the tingling between her legs to know just how much of a keeper he was. But he would be a keeper for some other woman, definitely not her. She frowned, wondering why the thought of that suddenly annoyed her.

Natalie began her checklist. "I don't have to ask if he's good in bed."

She couldn't help but laugh again. "No, please, don't bother."

"Okay, then. Is he someone you would want as a friend?"

A friend? Yes, she could see him being her friend once they put the bedroom behind them. But when she saw him, she didn't think of friendship, just sexual satisfaction. "Yes, he's someone I'd want as a friend."

"Okay, then. Do you consider yourself happy when you're with him?"

That was a no-brainer. Of course she was happy whenever she was with him. He could do things with his mouth, tongue and erection that could keep any woman delirious. "Definitely," she heard herself saying.

"Get your mind out of the bedroom, Langley, and provide responses on a purely plausible basis."

"Not sure I can do that with Xavier. Our relationship was one that started in the bedroom."

"That's not true. If anyone's relationship started in the bedroom, it was mine and Donovan's. Your relationship with Xavier started at Racetrack Café, Farrah. You were the one who was quick to carry it into the bedroom."

Farrah thought about Natalie's accusation and had to agree that she had been the one who'd instituted a sex-only relationship with Xavier from the first. Of course he had gone along with it. What man wouldn't have? She had known the moment she'd lit her gaze upon him that night that she'd wanted him.

"Sorry, but I've conditioned myself to only think one way when it comes to men. And please, please don't tell me again that all men aren't the same."

"Maybe if I keep saying it, one day you'll believe me."

"I believe that now, Nat, but like I said, I don't have the time to find out who's naughty and who's nice. I can't risk taking a chance and being wrong."

"I think deep down you want a man who's both naughty and nice and you have both with Xavier."

Farrah released a deep sigh. "What is this? Slapsome-sense-into-my-best-friend-where-Xavier-Kane-is-concerned Day?"

"I won't even try doing that. You'll have to see for yourself what a great guy he is."

"I hate to burst that romantic bubble floating around your heart, but all Xavier wants from me is sex, too. It's not that serious. Only problem with that is that I could fall in love with him, Nat, if I'm not careful and I can't let that happen. Thanks for listening." Not waiting for Natalie to reply, she quickly ended the call. "Love you. Bye."

Finding a more comfortable position in bed, she stared up at the ceiling again as she drew in a ragged breath. Sleep continued to elude her as one thought replayed in her head. A woman was entitled to make at least one mistake in her lifetime, but a smart woman wouldn't be a fool and make two.

Xavier slipped into his robe as he eased out of bed, unable to sleep. At this very moment he should have been in Farrah's bed making love to her again. When she'd ridden the elevator up to her room, he should have been on that elevator with her, kissing her every second of the ride.

Okay, so her refusal to jump-start their affair again had thrown him for a loop. He'd figured after tonight she would have seen the merit in them hooking back up. Evidently they weren't on the same page. Not even close.

Moving through the hallway, he walked down the

stairs to the kitchen. He had purchased this house on Long Island as investment property a few years ago and hadn't regretted doing so. He liked New York and whenever he came to town he much preferred staying here than in a hotel.

Grabbing a beer from the refrigerator, he slid onto a bar stool. The night was quiet, understandably so. Most sane people were in bed getting a good night's sleep. But not him. He was letting a woman tie him in knots.

He was in a bad way. Pretty messed up. Royally.

He took a huge gulp of his beer, acknowledging that he'd been delivered a setback. It wasn't the first time with a woman, but he'd never been this interested in one before. And to think that all she wanted was a holiday fling.

He took another swig of his beer while memories of their night together came tearing into him, and he couldn't help but recall when she'd gone down on him. And then later when his body had slid into hers, he'd felt as if he was someplace he could stay forever. Even stretched out as best she could on the car's backseat, she had used their limited space effectively and met him stroke for stroke. And as much as he wanted to chalk her up as a lost cause and move on with his life, he knew that he couldn't.

He knew it wasn't just about sex with Farrah, although that part of their relationship was always off the chart. But now when he took the time to think about it, it had always been more than just two bodies mating, at least in his book. She had a way of touching him everywhere and not just below the belt. From the first, he'd always felt in sync with her. Whenever she would smile, something inside of him would light up. And then there were those feelings of loneliness whenever he wasn't with her. For the past six months it had felt as if something was missing from his life. She was the only woman since Dionne who could fill him with emotions. Emotions he thought had died a hard death a long time ago.

He held his beer bottle to his lips, ready to take another healthy sip, when he was hit with a realization that had his heart pounding, his pulse racing and his esophagus tightening. This couldn't be happening to him. No way. But as he stared into space for a few seconds, he knew that it had already happened. He had fallen for Farrah and hard.

Damn.

What had happened to that strong resolve to guard his heart? What had happened to all those instilled and painful memories of what Dionne had done to him? He wasn't sure what had happened, but he knew, just as surely as he knew Diana Ross was once a Supreme, that he was in love with Farrah Langley.

He set his beer bottle down, thinking that definitely put a whole new spin on things. It hadn't been his intent to fall in love, but it had happened and now he planned to do something about it, which didn't include running in the other direction. No, he'd confront the opposition head on. This was his heart they were talking about.

He knew without being told that if she got wind of

his feelings, she would make things even more difficult. But he had news for her. Not only was he going to have his fling with her in the Big Apple, but it would continue right to Charlotte and eventually lead into marriage.

Marriage?

Yeah, marriage.

He smiled, thinking he liked the sound of that. He knew the hell she would probably give him, but he was up for the battle. All was fair in love and war, and he would do whatever it took to win her over and make her realize that regardless of what had happened in her past, he was the man for her.

It was a good thing Farrah wasn't there to see the sly smile that had formed around his lips. She wouldn't know what hit her until it was too late for her to do a damn thing about it.

Chapter 9

Farrah wasn't so sure how today's session with Kerrie Shaw and Lori Byers would pan out when Rudolph Byers strolled in by his wife's side with a smirk on his face, as if he knew something they all didn't. She couldn't help wondering if all the progress she'd made with the two women would get flushed down the toilet by the man who was determined to keep a wedge between the friends.

"Good morning, everyone, and welcome back," she said when they were all seated at the conference table. "I think we made really good progress yesterday and would like to pick up where we left off if everyone is in agreement." She held her breath, almost certain that Rudolph Byers would step in and oppose. When he did not and sat there beside his wife with that silly smirk still on his face, she continued.

"Okay, then, yesterday we ended with you, Kerrie, telling us about the early years when you and Lori worked together. Kerrie, I believe you were sharing with me how things were that first year when the two of you finished college."

Kerrie nodded, glanced over at Lori and smiled. Lori smiled back, which in Farrah's book was still a good sign. "Lori came up with this idea of how we could raise money for our first batch of makeup by getting a group of friends of ours in a band to agree to do a concert. ."

Farrah leaned back in her seat listening to what Kerrie was saying, while at the same time noticing there seemed to be a bit of tension between Lori and Rudolph. Being rude, he was doing annoying things to get his wife's attention as if to remind her that he was there. At first he'd been rubbing his finger up and down the sleeve of her blouse, and now he was entwining his fingers on the table with hers. It probably would have come off as a romantic gesture if he wasn't making it so obvious, so deliberate.

Moments later when Kerrie finished talking, Lori jumped in and said, "We used to have so much fun, although we operated in the red most of the time. I can recall when we finally were able to get out of Kerrie's parents' basement and into our own store in Queens."

"That was the store given to the two of you as a gift from your parents, right?"

"Yes, I guess they figured that was the least they could do after we bummed off the Shaws for almost two years," Lori said laughing.

Kerrie joined in the laughter, and she saw Rudolph Byers flinch as if the sound of the two women sharing memories of happier times bothered him. A half hour later Farrah called for a break and wasn't surprised when he pulled Lori off to the side. It wasn't hard to tell that whatever he was saying to her wasn't nice.

Moments later Lori frowned deeply before pulling away from him, and Farrah was grateful when the man stormed out of the conference room, slamming the door behind him.

Kerrie was on the other side of the room with her back to everyone while she talked on the phone, and the loud sound made her swirl around. An apologetic look appeared on Lori's face and she hunched her shoulders in disgust when she said, "Rudolph has an errand he needs to take care of and will be back after lunch."

The expression on Kerrie's face all but clearly said *good riddance*. Farrah refrained from saying anything, but she definitely agreed with Kerrie. She had the same opinion that she had yesterday. The man was bad news and a born manipulator.

Farrah glanced at her watch; it was still early. They had an hour and a half to go before they stopped for lunch. She couldn't help wondering what Xavier was doing. She had promised to call and let him know if she was free for dinner, and she would do so. She felt she needed to see him again since she knew their days together were numbered. She had thought about it, and to avoid being alone during the holidays, if he wanted to extend things until then, she would even consider that.

She began nibbling on her bottom lip wondering why she was doing this to herself. Why not make a clean break after she left here as she'd planned, instead of looking for any excuse to spend more time with him? Maybe one of the reasons was that she could remember the last holidays so well, and he had been a part of them.

It had been the best Christmas she had had in a long time, even better than the times when she'd been married to Dustin. But especially better than the year before when she'd been prepared to spend her holidays alone until Natalie had decided to come home.

The Steeles were a large family, and from talking to Natalie, she knew that this Christmas Donovan's parents, who traveled a lot since retiring, would be returning home for a huge family get-together. That meant, Farrah thought, that more than likely she would be spending the holidays alone.

If she were to suggest to Xavier that they continue their affair at least through the holidays, would he figure out why and grant her that request, or would he decide he didn't want to be used and tell her just where she could go? Besides, chances were he'd already made plans for the holidays.

She glanced across the room and noticed Kerrie had ended her phone call and was standing at the window looking out. Lori, standing on the other side of the room, appeared lost, and from her body language and expression, it was obvious she wanted to approach Kerrie but didn't know how to do so.

Farrah shook her head. Her heart truly went out to both women. Their relationship was badly in need of repair, and neither knew the best way of going about making it happen. "Ladies, I'm ready to resume things."

When both women sat down, she thought for a minute and then said, "You know I have a best friend, who, like the two of you, has been there for me since our high school years. There's nothing I wouldn't do for Natalie and there's nothing Natalie wouldn't do for me."

A smile touched the corners of Farrah's lips. "I know her secrets and she knows mine. She knows my weaknesses and my strengths and vice versa. We understand each other, which is why we've been friends for so long. We might not agree on everything, and I'm sure there have been times when she would have knocked my head off if she could have, but in the end, no matter what, I know our friendship is one that defies the test of time."

"I thought ours would, too," Lori said softly, looking at her when Farrah knew she wanted to glance over at Kerrie.

"I'm not going to ask what happened," Farrah said. "I just ask that no matter what, you remember what you had, what you still have and what will always be there no matter what."

At that moment, Lori did glance over at Kerrie. "You

think I'm only doing this because of Rudolph, don't you?"

Kerrie met her gaze and asked, "Why wouldn't I think it, Lori? Leaving the company in my hands was your idea. Saying that you would only want half up to the day you left was also yours. You also said that we keep things as they were to avoid any messy legal entanglements. It would be unnecessary, you said, since we fully trusted each other."

Kerrie shook her head and said softly, "The sad thing is that I believed you. Stupid me."

The room got quiet and Farrah spoke up. "Is this the first time your friendship has been tested?"

Both women glanced over at her with a bemused look on their faces, so much so that she couldn't help but smile. "You both know that's what this is, don't you?"

Neither woman made a comment, and Farrah figured she had given them something to think about. She glanced at her watch. "You know, I think now is a good time to break for lunch. It's a little early but I think we deserve it today."

Instead of responding, both women nodded as they stood. Kerrie was pulling out her cell phone while heading for the door. Lori watched her leave before turning to Farrah. She could see the tears in the woman's eyes.

"I didn't mean to hurt her," she said in a broken tone.

Farrah stood as she gathered her folders together. The last thing Lori needed was to be sent on a guilt trip, but in this case one was probably warranted. "Well, I hate to tell you this, Lori, but I think you did."

Xavier read the report spread across his desk and tried not to glance up at the clock on the wall. How many times had he done it already? He had to believe that eventually Farrah would call him. She'd said she would, hadn't she?

He threw the pencil he held in his hand down on his desk and leaned back in his chair as he squinted his eyes in thought, trying to recall exactly what she had said. *I'll call you tomorrow, Xavier. That's the best I can do.* Those had been her exact words. He recalled them clearly.

He was about to get up and pour another cup of coffee when his cell phone rang. If it was York, he was going to kill him. He'd called twice already. It seemed that York needed a life more than he did.

Xavier reached for the phone and exhaled a sigh of relief when he saw the caller was Farrah. He glanced at the clock. It was almost four. What had taken her so long? Of course he wouldn't ask her that. In fact, he intended to sound cool, calm and collected. "Hello."

"Xavier. Hi."

"And how are you, Farrah?"

"Fine. Sorry it took me so long to call but it turned out to be a long session today."

He nodded as he leaned back in his chair. "Did the women reach a resolution?"

"I wish."

"I take it that they didn't."

"You've got that right. But I can say I feel we're close. Hopefully tomorrow."

Not if it means you'll be catching the first plane out of here, he thought to himself.

"Anyway, I just wanted to let you know I'd love to have dinner with you."

He couldn't help the smile that touched his lips from corner to corner. "Good. Where are you now? Back at the hotel or still at work?"

"Still at work. I need to complete a few reports and then I'll head back to the hotel."

He glanced at the clock again. "Umm, how about around seven?"

"That's good."

"I'll send a car for you."

"A car?"

"Yes. I'm treating you to dinner at my place."

"In Long Island?"

"Yes."

There was a pause, and he waited, knowing she was rummaging through that gorgeous brain of hers for an excuse not to come. On cue she said, "You don't have to do that. I really don't want to put you through any trouble, Xavier. For me to come all the way to your place really isn't necessary."

Yes, it is, sweetheart. She had no idea just how necessary it truly was. "No trouble. Jules will be there to pick you up exactly at seven. I hope you're hungry."

She didn't say anything for a minute and then, "Yes, I'm hungry. I had a light lunch. But—"

"Good. I'll have something I know you'll like when you get here."

Another pause...and then, "Okay. Thanks."

"Don't mention it. I'll see you when you get here."

He closed his cell phone and placed it back on the desk where it had been since early morning, awaiting her call. Then he stood. It was time for him to go home and prepare dinner for the most lovable yet detached woman he knew. He planned to make things right for her or die trying.

He was well aware of why she assumed she didn't want another man in her life. His mission, which he fully intended to accept, was to convince her that she was worthy of everything life had to offer.

Especially his love.

Chapter 10

"Here we are, Ms. Langley."

"Thanks."

Jules offered Farrah his hand as she eased out of the car and glanced around. The huge triple-story house sat on what appeared to be a private lane, surrounded by a number of huge overhanging trees that formed a canopy over the impressive residence. If privacy was something Xavier was shooting for, then he had succeeded.

Pulling her coat tightly around her, she moved quickly toward the front door. She liked the sound of her booted heels as they clicked loudly against the stone pavers. She had lifted her hand to knock when the door opened.

Xavier was there, and she took a good look at him. He was eye candy of the most delicious kind. And dressed in a pullover sweater and low-riding jeans, he was the epitome of sexy. He moved out of her way as he invited her in. "Come on, I have a blaze roaring in the fireplace. I still intend to keep my promise to make sure you stay warm."

"I appreciate that."

As she followed him through his house, she noticed two things—the aroma of food cooking that made her mouth water, and the fact that he had a beautiful home. She knew this place was just one of many of his showplaces. He also had homes in Los Angeles, Miami and in the Palisades section of Charlotte, where houses went for millions. At least those were the ones he'd mentioned. There was no telling how many others he might own.

They passed a spiral staircase, and she couldn't help but glance up wondering if that was where his bedroom was and if she would find out for certain later. She shook her head. She needed to get her mind off sex, but that was definitely hard when, following him, she got an eyeful of the sexiest backside any man could possibly have.

By the time she'd reined in her wandering thoughts, she only caught his last word: *weather*.

"Excuse me, Xavier, what were you saying?"

He glanced over his shoulder, stopped walking and smiled. "I said it doesn't appear the weather is getting any better," he said, reaching for her hands. He removed her gloves and took her hands in his. As if he'd known they would be cold and stiff, he began massaging them.

Immediately, she felt heated sensations run through the tendons in her palms. The feelings were so strong she clenched her legs together when she felt an unexpected throbbing there.

No, the weather was not getting any better, which was quite obvious. The temperature had dropped, and depending on which news reports you were listening to, a snowstorm the likes of which New York hadn't seen in a long time was headed this way by Sunday. But Farrah knew that regardless of how cold it was outside, she would feel hot in here even if Xavier didn't have a fire roaring in the fireplace. Together, they could generate that kind of heat.

"Make yourself at home."

She broke eye contact with him and glanced around. They were in a room that he probably used as a den. It looked rustic with dark oak plank walls, the kind you'd find in a mountain cabin, and the fireplace was encased in whitewashed stone. The furniture looked sturdy and masculine, including the gigantic pool table in the middle of the room. He had mentioned that he enjoyed playing a game of pool every once in a while.

She glanced around the room again as she removed her coat, and as if he knew what she was thinking, he said, "No, I didn't decorate the place. It was bought as is. I figured the last owner wanted the feel of the Smoky Mountains in here, which is something I didn't have a problem with. In fact I think that's what enticed me to buy it."

She nodded as he came over and took the coat out of

her hands. She automatically eased down on the sofa, a little surprised she was still wearing clothes. She had really expected him to strip her naked the moment she had stepped over the threshold. It seemed he was going to take things slow. Slow was good. But if he started showing signs of wasting too much time, she knew how to take things into her own hands, literally. She inwardly smiled, thinking how she'd done that several times before.

"Here, you probably could use this to get your blood warm."

He handed her a glass filled with wine. When had he poured it? She took a sip, liking the sparkling taste, but then she'd always enjoyed his wine selections. She licked her lips and glanced across the room knowing he was watching her. That was good. Let him look. It would make things easier later when she threw her new idea out to him.

She cleared her throat. "Whatever you're cooking smells good, Xavier."

He chuckled. "Thanks, but I didn't cook it. Ms. Blackburn did it all."

She lifted a brow. "Ms. Blackburn?"

"Yes. My housekeeper, cook, gardener. You name it, she does it."

She lifted a brow again. "Umm, does she now?"

He laughed. "Except for that. For crying out loud, Farrah, she's old enough to be my mother. But I would admit to coming close to asking her to marry me one day after eating a slice of her apple pie."

"It was that delicious?"

"Honey, delicious doesn't come close."

She swallowed. No one could say the word delicious quite the way he could, and no one could do things deliciously quite like him. She'd bet no one could even come close.

"So, will you be meeting with those women again tomorrow since no closure came about today?"

She glanced over at him. He had moved to sit on a bar stool. His taut thighs strained tightly against the denim of his jeans, and his abs were outlined in his form-fitting sweater. Not an inch of flab anywhere. She knew in reality he much preferred beer to wine, but unlike some men, he didn't have a belly to show it.

And speaking of his belly…she thought he had a nice looking one, especially when it wasn't covered with clothes. She remembered quite well how a sprinkling of dark hair adorned it. And then there was that trail of hair that tapered off to his groin area. She felt her mouth watering again, and it wasn't for anything his housekeeper had left cooking on the stove.

She took a sip of her wine before saying, "Yes, I'll be meeting with them, but if everything continues in the same way as today, I'm hoping we'll wrap up by tomorrow. But that depends on—"

"One of the women's husband's involvement," he finished for her.

She nodded and smiled. "You remembered."

"Yes."

"And here I thought you were listening just to humor me and weren't really paying attention."

He met her gaze and held it. "I'm sure since we've met that you've made a number of assumptions about me that aren't true, Farrah."

She blinked, surprised he would say that. "Like what?"

"You'll find out soon enough."

She wondered what he meant by that. But then she would admit that maybe she had made a few assumptions. Being here in his home challenged one of them. She had always assumed his home, his domain, was off-limits to any woman. He'd never said that, but given the way he'd meticulously made his booty calls, she'd certainly thought so.

Xavier stood and placed his wine glass on the counter. She couldn't help the way her gaze followed his movement, especially the muscles in his thighs when they stretched. He was definitely a man who could wear a pair of jeans. But then he looked damn good in a business suit as well. And Lordy, she didn't want to think about how good he looked naked.

She blinked again, noticing his lips move. He was saying something. "Excuse me?"

He smiled, and she felt a tingle that seemed to take life in her stomach. Why did he have to have such a luscious mouth? And why did she have to remember all the things that mouth could do?

"I asked if you were ready for dinner."

She was ready for whatever he had in mind. Holding

back that thought, she cleared her throat and said instead, "Yes, just lead the way."

She followed him, appreciating another chance to check out his broad shoulders and the best backside a man could possess.

Xavier glanced across the table at Farrah and decided he was going to enjoy every single plan he put into action to win her over. They were almost finished with dinner, and just in case she planned to leave any time soon, he would suggest that she stick around to help with kitchen cleanup. He glanced back down at his plate thinking she didn't have to know Ms. Blackburn had instructed him to leave everything for her to take care of in the morning.

"You should have warned me, Xavier."

He glanced back up and met her gaze. The eyes staring back at him were a serious brown. He wondered if she'd figured out his action plan for tonight. "Warned you about what?"

"That I would be so full after this meal that you'd probably have to roll me out the door."

A relieved smile touched his lips. "I did warn you. I told you how I felt after eating her apple pie."

"I thought you were exaggerating. Now I see that you weren't. I've never eaten pork chops that all but melt in your mouth. They are so tender."

He had to agree, Ms. Blackburn had done a great job with dinner. And Farrah, he thought, had done a great job with dressing. She looked good tonight. When she'd taken off her coat, his tongue had almost wrapped around his head. That was one sexy purple dress she was wearing. It was short, which showed off her legs that were encased in tights and another pair of black leather knee-high boots. He had invited her over for dinner, not to give him heart failure.

"You look nice tonight, by the way."

She smiled at his compliment. "Thanks. You look good yourself."

He pushed his empty plate aside to lean back in his chair. "Glad you think so."

"I do. Always."

She was flirting with him, and as a man, he could only appreciate it. "Would you like some dessert now?" He watched her lick her lips, and he couldn't help but shift in the chair to ease the pressure behind his zipper.

"Sounds tempting but I'll wait for a while. I'd like to talk to you about something."

He wondered what she wanted to talk about. "Sure. Let's go in the family room and sit in front of the fireplace."

"But what about the dinner dishes?"

He smiled. "We can leave them for now and you can help me clean up the kitchen later."

"All right. That's the least I can do after such a wonderful meal."

No, that wasn't the least she could do, but he would keep that little tidbit to himself.

He rounded the table to pull the chair back for her. One thing he'd liked about Farrah from the first was that she never got offended when he did gentlemanly things for her. No matter how raw and raunchy they got in the bedroom, he totally enjoyed treating her like the lady he knew she was.

And she was a downright sexy lady at that, he thought as his gaze swept over her, up and down her body. Just looking at her almost derailed any thoughts about what was the best way to handle her. He wanted to get out of her the one thing he decided most important. For her to return his love.

He knew that was a tall order, one that would take measured, strategic planning. His goal was to convince her that he was a viable candidate for her affections, and that he was more husband material than her ex ever was.

When she walked off swaying her hips, it took all of his control not to reach out and pull her into his arms and begin removing every stitch of clothing she had on her body before tearing off his. Then it would be on, all over the place. His erection throbbed just thinking about it.

He momentarily closed his eyes while telling himself to hold tight and keep a handle on his control. It would all be worth it in the end, even though not making love to her tonight was going to drive him insane, especially when she was intentionally trying to bait him.

Xavier reopened his eyes the moment she glanced over her shoulder at him with a teasing smile on her face. "Are you coming, Xavier?"

He gave her a warning frown. He would definitely

be coming if she kept it up, but he intended to resist her temptation, even if it killed him. And he had a feeling that if it did kill him, he would die an excruciating, slow death. "I'm right behind you."

And he was. As she led the way back to his family room, he was what he considered a safe distance behind her, which had its advantages if you were into ass-watching. He was, especially when that part of the anatomy was hers.

She slid down on his sofa in a movement so fluid, so damn enticing, he didn't even blink as he watched her. He waited until she was settled in her seat before crossing the room and taking the recliner across from her. He'd known resisting her wouldn't be easy, but he hadn't counted on it being such torture. The woman was almost too hot for his own good.

He cleared his throat. "So, what do you want to talk about?"

"Us."

Us? She'd never referred to them as an *us,* so in a way things sounded pretty good already. "I'm listening."

She began nibbling on her lower lips. He knew that sign. Whatever topic she wanted to broach wasn't easy for her. "I, um, I was thinking about what you said last night."

He'd said a lot of things. He'd done a lot of things, too. "And?"

"And you wanted us to continue the affair past New York."

Had she come around without much prodding from him? "Yes, I recall having said that."

She began nibbling on her lips again, and then she said, "I'd like to offer a proposal to you."

He lifted a brow. "A proposal?"

"Yes."

He leaned back in the chair as he rubbed his jaw. This had better be good, he thought. It'd better be what he wanted. "I'm listening."

"I don't have any plans for the holidays and I thought…"

She paused, but he was determined that she finish what she was saying. "You thought what, Farrah?"

She met his gaze while nibbling those luscious lips again. "That since you wanted to continue things between us for a while, that we could extend our affair at least through New Year's."

He didn't say anything. He had to make sure he fully understood what she was offering. "Are you saying that once you leave here it's okay for us to hook up in Charlotte again, with things being like they used to be with us?"

She nodded. "Yes, but only through the holidays."

He ignored the ache in his body that tried convincing him that something was better than nothing, and that he should take her up on her offer. But he wasn't in the market for just being involved in a holiday affair. He wanted the whole shebang. That meant he had no intention of letting her place limitations on their relationship.

"So, what do you think?"

He shrugged his shoulders and wondered if she was prepared for what he was about to say. "I think I'll pass."

Voices in his head were calling him all kinds of fool for not accepting her offer. One voice in particular was all but giving his brain a hard kick, screaming that if he thought he could convince her to consider a real relationship with him, he was crazy and wasting his time. Her ex had done too much of a number on her for that to happen. How many times had she told him that she would never, ever, become involved in a serious relationship again? How many times had she reiterated that fact for his benefit?

"You'll pass?" she asked, with a mixture of shock and confusion outlining what he thought were gorgeous features. "But why?"

He held her gaze. "Because I told you what I wanted."

"For us to pick up where we left off?"

"Yes, and continue from there without any limitations, Farrah."

She shook her head. "That's not going to work, Xavier. That's why I thought it was best if we ended things six months ago."

"Whatever hang-ups there were, Farrah, were yours, not mine. The only reason I gave into it at the time was because I convinced myself that perhaps you were right. After last night I decided you're dead wrong."

The flaring of fire in her eyes let him know she hadn't

appreciated what he'd just said. It didn't take a rocket scientist to know he'd pushed the wrong button, but at the moment he really didn't give a damn. It was time they had it out. He refused to go through another long spell without her.

She leaned forward in her seat. "This new attitude of yours is all because of last night? One good blow job got you all up in arms? Got you refusing a holiday fling with me because you want more than that?"

He slid out the chair to stand on his feet. "It's more than that, Farrah, and you know it. It's about the chemistry we stir whenever we're together. I see nothing wrong with wanting more. But after almost a year, you decided we should end things. Why? Because you had begun feeling something a lot deeper and more solid than mere orgasms."

"That's not true!" she said adamantly.

"Isn't it?"

"It was just sex, Xavier. You could have gotten the same from any woman."

"Hardly, which is why I haven't slept with another woman since you. And probably why you haven't, by your admission, been intimate with anyone since me."

He thought he'd hit a nerve, and she proved him right when she began pacing angrily. He decided to sit back in the chair and let her blow off steam, come to terms with being called out. Except he was getting more turned on by the second watching her, seeing how the hair was flying around her face with every livid step she took in boots that were definitely made for more than walking.

Her hips were not just swaying now, they were being brandished about under the sting of rejection. Something she evidently didn't care much for. Not for the first time, he noticed just how small her waist was, and how her hips flared out in an almost perfect womanly shape. And her breasts—heaven help him, they were the most luscious pair on any woman—were straining against the bodice of her dress.

While his gaze roamed all over her, she finally came to a stop mere inches from where he sat. She placed her hands on her hips. "So, what exactly is it that you want?"

He smiled and leaned forward in his chair and met her gaze without wavering. He fought the urge to tell her that what he wanted was marriage, until death do them part. Considering everything, he figured now was not a good time to share that with her.

"What I want is for us to resume our affair without limitations. That means we go for as long as we're mutually satisfied."

She rolled her eyes. "People only do long-term affairs when they want to get serious eventually. People who want more out of a relationship. People who might even contemplate marriage."

"Not necessarily. I think we know each other's position on marriage, so we don't have to worry about us wanting anything *that* serious. However, I'm at a point in my life where I prefer long-term exclusiveness. Not only do I want a satisfying bed partner, I also want to be with someone I can take out to dinner on occasion, to a movie, to those business functions that I'm oftentimes invited to attend. I don't like women coming on to me anymore. I want to emit an air that I'm taken…even if I'm truly not."

He paused, wanting her to digest what he'd just said. Then he continued. "You enjoy my company and I enjoy yours. I see no reason why we can't continue what we had unless…"

She tilted her head and looked at him, lifting a brow. "Unless what?"

"Unless you're afraid of falling in love with me."

He eased up from his seat, ignoring the burst of longing and love he felt for the woman standing in front of him. The woman he was determined to make fall in love with him to the same degree that he was with her.

He knew now that she wasn't as opposed to restarting their affair as she put on. But she was scared of letting her heart get broken again. So he knew he had to tread lightly but at the same time push harder…if that made sense.

"Are you afraid, Farrah? If you are, then I understand and totally agree that we should not pick up where we left off."

He immediately saw the effect his words had on her. After her jaw dropped to the floor, she went still. He was convinced she was barely breathing. And her gaze intensified, focused on him. Her eyes zeroed in on him

like he was the only thing in their laser beam's target.
From the distance separating them, he felt her anger,
but he also felt her fear. He actually saw it in her eyes,
and he knew at that moment what he'd assumed was
right. She was falling in love with him, but was fighting
it tooth and nail. She would never, ever admit such a
thing.

So he stood there watching her, waiting to see how
she planned on getting out of the neat little box he'd just
placed her in.

Chapter 11

Think, Farrah!

She nibbled on her bottom lip as she tried unscrambling her brain, refusing to admit Xavier had hit a nerve, which automatically put her on the defensive. "Me? Not being able to control my emotions and fall in love? Please. That is the last thing you, or any man, have to worry about, trust me."

He shrugged. "If you say so."

She didn't like the sound of that. Did he honestly think she'd fall in love with him? Okay, she would admit—although never to him—that she had ended things between them because she'd had feelings for him and had been uncomfortable with those newfound emotions. But she would never let any man suspect she was afraid of losing her heart.

She threw her head back, sending her hair flying over her shoulders. "I'm going to only say this once and I hope you're listening, Xavier. The last thing you have to worry about, and the one thing I am *not* afraid of, is falling in love with you or any man. I've been there, done that and you can believe I'll never go that way again."

"In that case, I see no reason for us not to continue our affair beyond the holidays. In other words, there is no reason not to go back to things being the way they were. And in addition, I see no reason why we can't bring our affair out of the bedroom and start going out more…unless there's a reason you prefer not being seen with me."

Farrah's head was spinning dizzily with everything Xavier was saying. But she was coherent enough to latch on to his last statement. "For what reason would I not want to be seen with you?"

"That you're still pining away for your ex-husband and you don't want him to know you're in a relationship with someone."

If Farrah hadn't been programmed to act in a dignified manner, especially when discussing such an important topic, she would have fallen to the floor and rolled over a few times in laughter. Anyone who knew her and Dustin's history knew there was no way that she was pining for her ex. In fact, whenever she saw him, she wondered why she'd fallen in love with him in the first place. It's not that he'd ever had anything going for him that was so spectacular. But while they'd been in college, he had convinced her he was the best thing since sliced bread and that he would be going places.

She had believed he loved her, wanted to spend the rest of his life with her and they would stay together forever. She didn't even mind during their first year when he couldn't get a job and she had supported the both of them, or the times she'd put up with his deadbeat parents whose way of life was calling for loans and not paying them back.

"So, did I hit it out of the ballpark, Farrah?"

She could only assume he figured that because she hadn't yet responded to his statement. "You didn't come close, Xavier. In fact, you struck out so bad they are replacing you in the game entirely. There is no way I'd ever get back with Dustin, nor do I want to."

She didn't like the look she saw in his eyes. Although he heard what she said, she couldn't tell if he believed her.

"*If* what you say is true, then there is no reason why we can't continue what we once had without limitations, right?"

Farrah's pulse began beating wildly, anxiously, and that cloak of protectiveness she used as a shield immediately went into place. There were lots of reasons why they couldn't continue what they once had. And not imposing limitations was simply out of the question.

Although she would never admit she had developed a weakness for him, the truth of the matter was that on more than one occasion she had lost control and lowered her guard, which was totally unacceptable behavior. When she was with Xavier she had a tendency to let loose, getting buck wild and crazy. Not just in the bedroom—that she could handle. But with her heart. Only with him did she care about the here and now and not worry about the outcome.

She lifted her chin. "There *is* a reason," she said, knowing what she was about to say was an absolute lie. "Have you ever considered that the only reason I don't want to take up where we left off in an affair, Xavier, is because I just don't want to be romantically involved with you any longer?"

Darn. Instead of frowning, he was smiling, which meant he hadn't believed a word she'd just said. Hadn't taken her seriously. She watched as he crossed his arms over his chest and braced his legs apart in a ready-for-combat stance. She hated thinking it, but his standing that way and looking at her with that "I know better" smirk on his face sent a rush of adrenaline up her spine.

"You expect me to believe that, Farrah? The same woman who I took on the backseat of a private car last night while cruising on a barge on an icy cold night down the Hudson."

She narrowed her eyes at him. "Why can't I convince you it was nothing but sex?"

He shrugged his shoulders. "I don't know, but here's your chance. Convince me. Prove you're not afraid of letting your emotions get in the way of an affair with me, and that your mind is not getting confused with the L-word. Prove to me, Farrah, that for us it's only about sex, which is the only thing we want anyway, and that we don't have to worry about anything else to the point that we establish limitations."

Her mind was spinning in confusion, and she wondered if he'd caused that to happen deliberately. All she knew at that moment was that she had a point to prove to him, several in fact. First, she was capable of keeping her emotions under wraps. Second, she was not still carrying a torch for Dustin. And last but not least, she was not afraid of falling in love with Xavier.

"Fine," she threw out heatedly. "You think you've got everything figured out, but I'm going to prove you wrong, Xavier. I'm going to give you your affair without limitations and then you're going to see just how wrong you are about everything."

Xavier couldn't ignore the burst of happiness that tore through him at that moment, and he had to fight hard to keep a smile off his lips. With some outright manipulation, which he wasn't all that thrilled about, he had moved Farrah into the spot where he wanted her for now.

She had agreed to an affair without limitations, and he doubted that she fully understood exactly what that meant, but she would find out soon enough. Although they would continue to make love just as before, they would not be spending one hundred percent of the time between the sheets. He would take her out on dates, to parties—there were always a number of them to attend this time of year—and she would get to spend time with him around people who meant a lot to him. They were family and friends who would come to love her as much as he did.

"Good, we're on the same page now," he heard himself saying as he crossed the room to her, needing to feel her in his arms, although he could tell she was still somewhat tiffed with him.

"Fine," she said, when he slid his arm around her waist and brought her body closer to his. She might not be happy with him now, but the moment he pulled her into his arms, she came willingly. And when he lowered his head to capture her mouth, there was not a single ounce of resistance in her body.

She leaned in, and he felt her warmth deep, all the way to the pit of his stomach. He wasn't surprised when he felt the shiver ease up his spine and his erection get harder. Desire sizzled through him, and he fought to push it back. This woman could set his body on fire, and at any other time he would take advantage of it. But not this time. He had his game plan tonight and didn't want to ruin it.

But there was no reason he couldn't make love to her mouth if not her body, was there? After all, when it came to kissing, they always indulged in the ultimate enjoyment. Then he remembered. The fact that he had managed to breathe six months without tasting her was a miracle, and he didn't intend to suffer through that agony again.

He finally pulled his mouth away, but their greedy tongues were still intent on doing a tangling dance, if not inside their mouths then out. They always enjoyed this type of play where they took licking and sucking to a whole new level.

And then his tongue was back inside her mouth again, and his arms tightened around her. It wouldn't take much to ease her down on the sofa, push her dress up, pull down those leggings and bury his head between her legs and do a lot of tongue play there. It wouldn't take much enticement for him to kiss every inch of her body. Unfortunately, he would save that specific activity for another day. Unknown her to, this kind of kissing was all they would be doing tonight.

Ah hell, he thought, when he felt her hands wiggle between them and her fingers tug on his zipper. He needed to stop her before she went down on him. There was no way he could resist that. With all the strength he could gather, all the control he could muster, he reached down and took hold of her hand to stop her from going further.

She pulled her mouth from his and looked up at him with a questioning gaze. "Why are you holding my hands, Xavier?"

Before answering her question, he leaned down and took another lick around her mouth. Hell, she tasted as good as she looked. "I want to give you time to be absolutely sure I'm what you want, Farrah."

He had worded the statement carefully. Instead of saying he wanted her to be sure that the *affair* was what she wanted, he had said he wanted her to be sure that *he* was what she wanted. There was a difference, and over the next few weeks he would show her what that difference was.

"But I already know you're what I want, Xavier."

Yes, she would want him sexually, that was a given. But he wanted her to want him in a way she'd never wanted another man, a way that went deeper than mere sex. He wanted to conquer her heart. For a man who just last week had thought he didn't need the love of a woman, in the last forty-eight hours he had been proven wrong.

"Yes, but I want you to be certain because now that you've agreed to an unlimited affair with me, Farrah, there's no turning back."

She lifted her brow, as if his comment gave her pause. "No turning back" sounded kind of final in his book, so he knew it sounded likewise in hers, but now he was talking for keeps.

She didn't say anything for a long moment and then, "Why are you trying to make things so complicated, Xavier?"

"Sorry if you think I'm doing that, sweetheart, but I just want to make sure a few weeks from now you don't try kicking me out of your life again. I have to know that we want the same thing out of this relationship."

He was trying to defuse any suspicions she had that things with him weren't on the up-and-up. He only hoped when she discovered they weren't she would be too far gone to care.

She nodded slowly. "Okay, I guess that makes sense."

"It does. Besides, another reason I need to make it an early night is because Cameron is flying in tomorrow and I need to have some papers ready for him to sign when he does."

He was deliberately giving her the impression that he was putting work before her. Although she didn't say anything, he could tell she was both surprised and disappointed.

"Oh, well, then I guess I need to go."

"Not before we share dessert and not before you help me with kitchen clean up."

She smiled. "All right."

He wanted to kiss her again, and he figured before she left to return to the hotel that he would, several times. But at least she would be leaving with the knowledge that for the first time, though they'd had the convenience and the privacy to make love, they hadn't.

"Is the car warm enough for you, Ms. Langley?"

Farrah glanced over the seat in front of her at Jules. Xavier had given the driver strict instructions to see to her every comfort, and to especially make sure she was kept warm.

"Yes, thank you for asking."

She settled back against the plush leather seat, determined to replay in her mind all that had transpired tonight and to make sure she hadn't imagined anything.

She'd gone to his house fully intending to convince

him to extend their affair through the holidays, after which, they would go their separate ways again.

For reasons she was still trying to figure out, he hadn't wanted any part of that suggestion. Instead, he wanted to resume the affair with no limitations. He'd even gone so far as to suggest her reluctance to do so was because she was afraid of falling in love with him and because she still harbored feelings for Dustin.

Okay, secretly she would agree the former did have some merit, but the latter did not. To prove him wrong on both counts, she had no choice but to agree to his terms. So technically, they were now involved in a long-term, no-strings relationship.

Even more confusing to her was how, once she'd agreed, their relationship had taken a definite turn. But to where she hadn't a clue. First, it had been the way he'd kissed her. It was greedy and hungry as usual, but it seemed like he was holding back, which didn't make sense. After all, she had agreed to what he'd wanted. And no matter what she'd done, she hadn't changed his mind about sleeping with her, although she knew without a doubt that he'd wanted her.

Men!

Now here she was, riding in the car alone as she returned to her hotel. Truly, what sense did that make? He could have easily asked that she stay the night and she would have. But he hadn't. He'd even suggested she take time to think her decision through. Now, drawing in a deep breath, she decided to do just what he'd suggested.

As the car sped along the Long Island Expressway, she closed her eyes. An unlimited affair with him meant essentially no more booty calls. At least they wouldn't be termed that anymore. She had agreed that she and Xavier would start doing things outside the bedroom. More than likely they would go out to dinner on occasion, to a movie, to business functions.

She felt a knot forming in the pit of her stomach at the thought of doing those things with him and knew the reason why. She might just begin to enjoy it too much. Her challenge was going to be keeping things in perspective. Though neither of them wanted to take things any further than they had previously, Xavier was now ready for more exclusiveness. At least she could rest assured he still wasn't the marrying kind. Good, she thought, because neither was she.

She opened her eyes and glanced down at her watch. It wasn't even midnight. Depending on how things turned out between Kerrie Shaw and Lori Byers, she could very well be back in Charlotte around this time tomorrow. Doing so would have her out of New York before the snowstorm hit on Sunday. Xavier had even offered to take her to the airport tomorrow. Getting back home might be a good thing. It would put distance between them for at least a week and would give her time to clear her head and decide on the best way to handle him.

Over ice cream and apple pie, Xavier had told her about his trip after the holidays to Los Angeles where he would be for a few days in January. Usually, she wouldn't know about his trips until he was packed and ready to go because that was the type of relationship they'd had. For him to keep her abreast of his plans was going to take some getting used to.

But for now she wanted just to concentrate on what had or hadn't happened tonight. Sex was one of the things that hadn't happened, and for a reason she didn't quite understand. A part of her believed it was intentional on Xavier's part.

She had come here fully expecting dinner followed by hot, mind-blowing sex. That was the only kind she'd ever shared with Xavier, and tonight she had been willing, but for some reason, he had held back.

After dessert he had kissed her a few times, and although she would admit the kisses had been long, drugging and delicious enough to tingle her toes and wet her panties, she had still felt him holding back on her. It was as if he was keeping himself in check, fearful of just what too many slow, deep kisses could do to them.

And then, after they'd cleaned up the kitchen together, he had helped her back into her coat and gloves, had picked her up in his arms and, instead of carrying her upstairs to a bedroom, he had carried her outside and placed her on the backseat of the private car.

He had told her that regardless of whether she stayed in New York over the weekend, he would be seeing her tomorrow and to expect his call. Why was she thinking already that, in addition to the feel of him easing back off sex, she was also losing control of the relationship? Now it seemed as if he had taken the lead role in managing just how things went between them.

And she wasn't sure if she particularly liked giving any man that much control over her.

"We'll be at your hotel in less than five minutes, Ms. Langley," the driver interrupted her thoughts to inform her.

"Thanks, Jules."

As they drove into the city, she wondered what would be the best way to take back that control she had somehow lost tonight. She didn't like any man calling the shots and had dispensed with that nonsense at the moment the ink had dried on her divorce papers from Dustin.

After the divorce she had been furious, even resentful, and at one point out for blood. In a fit of spite, she'd thought about suing the other woman. North Carolina was one of a few states that still enforced a century-old case law that said a wife could sue her husband's mistress for breaking up a marriage. Her attorney had been more than happy to do it, and Dustin's attorney had scared her ex-husband shitless by informing him of a recent suit in which the duped ex-wife had gotten nine million dollars richer. Natalie had talked her out of it, but still she'd felt good knowing she had made Dustin sweat for a while.

When the driver brought the car to a stop in front of her hotel, she gathered up her things. She had been so certain about tonight that she'd put her toothbrush in her purse. In a way, she was somewhat disappointed. But then she would be the first to admit engaging in the unknown was kind of exciting. She couldn't help wondering what Xavier had planned for tomorrow. Surely he wasn't going to push for another wasted night. If he did try going that route, she would have to do something about it.

Chapter 12

"Hey, man, you okay?"

Xavier glanced across the desk at Cameron thinking that if he looked like a man who'd had a sleepless night then that was definitely right on the money. After he'd put Farrah inside the car and sent her home, he had walked around his house with a hard-on that wouldn't go down. He'd called himself all kinds of fool. Although he'd known that in the long run he had done the right thing for them, he'd gone to bed with regrets of not having made love to her.

"No, not really," he said, deciding to be honest.

The necessary documents had been signed, and now Cameron Cody owned yet another company. The negotiations had gone well, better than expected. Sleep-deprived or not, when it came to business, Xavier knew he was on top of his game. But now that he and Cameron were alone, that adrenaline high from earlier was fizzling fast.

"What's your problem, Xavier?"

He couldn't help but smile at Cameron's question. For the first time since Dionne, he was actually having a problem with a woman. Before, he'd never considered a female significant enough to cause a problem in his life, but with Farrah things were different.

"I have a lot of decisions to make and I want to be absolutely sure I'm making the right ones."

Cameron leaned back in his seat and chuckled. "I assume these decisions are about Farrah Langley."

Xavier raised a brow. He'd never discussed Farrah with anyone, although he was certain after Donovan's wedding a number of his friends—his godbrothers in particular—had figured he and Farrah were involved in a hot and heavy affair. "How did you know?"

Cameron chuckled. "Because I know you. You started paying late-night visits to the same woman on a rather frequent basis. And since you never discussed these visits or the woman with me or anyone, that was the first sign."

"Sign?"

"Yes, a sign that this particular woman meant something to you and that you thought she was different from all the others."

Xavier nodded slowly. Yes, Farrah was different from the others. At first he'd just enjoyed being in her bed, but then something had begun happening to him, although at first he hadn't known exactly what. It had taken half a year of not being with her to make him realize Farrah was more than a woman he just wanted in his bed. Once he'd seen her again, spent time with her, he'd known she was the only woman he wanted in his life for always. "I'm crazy about her, Cam," he admitted.

"Does she know how you feel?"

Xavier shook his head. "Hell, I just figured it out myself a few days ago. We broke up a week after Donovan's wedding—her idea, not particularly mine. She thought our short-term affair had gone on longer than intended and it was time to move on. I didn't argue and will admit at the time I thought maybe she was right. And then a couple of days ago we ran into each other here in New York. She's in town on business like I am. We went out to dinner that first night and a Broadway play the next. I enjoyed her company and realized just how much I had missed her. Then I knew exactly what had been truly missing from my life for the past six months."

Cameron smiled. "Now you can understand why I wouldn't let up in my pursuit of Vanessa, although it didn't take me as long as it took you to figure out I was in love, and that Vanessa was the woman I wanted in my life."

"Um, that might be true, but I have a feeling I'm going to work just as hard to win her over," Xavier said. He paused, thinking of all the things Cameron had done during his pursuit of Vanessa, and then shook his head and laughed. "Hell, I hope not."

Cameron couldn't help laughing as well. "But in the end it was all worth it."

All Xavier had to do was to see them together to know what Cameron said was true. "I'm definitely in love with Farrah, Cam." Xavier wasn't surprised how easily the words flowed from his lips.

"Good. I like her, so what's the problem?" Cameron asked.

Xavier sighed deeply. After all Cameron had gone through for Vanessa, if anyone understood his plight, it would be him. "She can't seem to get over a bad marriage. Her husband cheated on her and ended up marrying the other woman. He even went so far as to have a child with her while married to Farrah."

Cameron shook his head sadly. "Some bastards really make it hard for the rest of us, don't they?"

Xavier nodded in agreement. Farrah's ex was making it nearly impossible for him. "Yes, it's going to be difficult for her to trust another man."

"Be patient. Some scars are harder to heal than others."

Xavier understood that. It had taken him years to get over the damage Dionne had done to him. But he truly believed in his heart that Farrah and Dionne were nothing alike, and now he had to prove that fact to Farrah.

"I'm sure you have a plan, Xavier."

Xavier chuckled. Cameron knew him well enough to know just how he operated. "Yes. Last night I got her to agree to resume our affair with no limitations. That in itself wasn't an easy task, so I feel good about it. The next thing I intend to do is prove to her that there's more between us than just great sex."

Farrah had expected to get carted off to his bed last night. He could tell. A part of him believed she was somewhat confused as to why he hadn't slept with her. She had tried more than once to tempt him, and he'd known exactly what she was doing. A few times his traitorous body had almost given in, but luckily his ironclad control had ruled.

"Thanks for listening to my woes, Cam."

"Hey, no problem. That's what friends are for. Now, I'm out of here. That snow storm they had predicted for Sunday is blowing in early, and I intend to be gone before then."

Xavier glanced out the window, noticing for the first time the weather had changed. The sky was white and heavy, the wind blustery. He needed to call Farrah to see if she planned to leave for Charlotte today. A smile touched his lips. Although he knew it would be a bad idea with all the temptation she would present, he kind of liked the idea of her getting snowed in, in the city. Of course he would invite her to move in with him until the worst of the storm passed. He could imagine how it would be if that were to happen.

"What are you smiling about, Xavier?"

He glanced up at Cameron. "Trust me, you don't want to know."

"I've made a decision about things, Ms. Langley."

Farrah glanced over at Lori. Her husband hadn't come

with her today, and as far as Farrah was concerned, that was a good sign. She wondered if today would entail another long, drawn out session. They had covered a lot of ground yesterday, revisited a lot of memories, and Farrah hoped doing so had worked.

"And what decision is that, Lori?"

"That I'm fine with a seventy-thirty split. Kerrie's right in thinking that I don't deserve fifty-fifty. Besides, I admit to telling her that years ago, and I won't go back on my word now. Our friendship means more to me than that."

Kerrie glanced over at Lori. "I think you deserve more than seventy-thirty Lori. I'm willing to go back to the original contract between us and honor that."

Lori shook her head. "I won't let you do that. I walked away from the business. You're the one who made it into what it is today, and I won't be greedy about it."

Kerrie then asked, "What about Rudolph? How will he feel about it?"

Lori shrugged. "I told him my decision this morning. He's not happy about it, but it was my decision to make. He'll just have to get over it since this doesn't really concern him. These past few days have made me realize that the business was based on our friendship, our trust and love for each other. I can't let anyone destroy those things."

Farrah couldn't help but admire Lori for the decision she'd made and for standing up to her husband. She wondered if it was the first time Lori had defied him. "Well, I'm glad we've resolved the matter, and I'll get the papers ready to be signed so we can all leave before the weather worsens. It looks like it's about to start snowing any minute."

"It does," Lori said in agreement. "And I want to thank you for reminding me that true friendship will outlast anything, and that's what Kerrie and I have always had."

Kerrie nodded in agreement before reaching across the table and taking Lori's hand in hers.

Farrah drew in a deep breath, feeling good about the resolution and happy about how things had worked out in the end. She glanced at her watch, wondering if she would be able to get a flight out today before the storm hit.

An hour or so later she checked her phone and saw she'd received a text message from Xavier. All it said was—Cold outside. Car will pick you up.

Moments later when she exited the building, she saw his private car parked at the curb waiting for her. Jules smiled when he saw her and quickly opened the car door. "Mr. Kane sent me with instructions to take you wherever you want to go, Ms. Langley."

Farrah smiled as she slid onto the backseat. It was cold, and she couldn't help but appreciate the vehicle's warmth. "Please take me to my hotel. I want to get a flight out before the storm arrives."

At that minute her phone rang. She smiled when she saw it was Xavier and immediately clicked on the call. "Xavier, thanks for sending the car."

"I promised to keep you warm, didn't I?"

Her smile widened. "Yes."

"So did things get resolved today?"

"Yes," she said excitedly. "I feel good in not only resolving another case, but with this particular one, renewing a friendship. Now I'm headed back to the hotel to pack. The storm's coming and I'm afraid if I don't get a flight out today, I might get stranded here."

"I hate to tell you this but you might already be stranded. I heard on the news that they've already started canceling flights headed to New York, which means that flights leaving the city are being impacted."

Farrah frowned, disappointed. "The last thing I want is to get stranded here."

"In that case you might be in luck. Cameron is here and will be flying out in his private plane in a few hours. If you're ready to leave, then you can fly back to Charlotte with him."

Farrah blinked. "I can't impose on Mr. Cody like that, Xavier. He doesn't know me that well."

Xavier laughed. "Cam knows you're a close friend of mine. I'll make the necessary arrangements with him. You just get packed. I'll touch base with you in an hour."

Farrah clicked off the phone, thinking just how appreciative she would be if Xavier could arrange for her to leave New York before the storm hit. But to accompany Cameron Cody in his private plane, she thought, was asking too much. Although he and his wife were Natalie's cousins-in-law, as she'd told Xavier, she didn't want to impose on the man.

She shook her head, somewhat disappointed. If she left the hotel and went straight to the airport, that would mean she wouldn't see Xavier before leaving. Nor had he said anything about wanting to see her again before she left.

"We're here, Ms. Langley."

Farrah pushed her disappointment aside. This had turned out to be a happy day, and she refused to let thoughts of Xavier put a damper on it.

Xavier couldn't ignore the shiver of pleasure that ran down his spine when Jules pulled the car up in front of Farrah's hotel. And then moments later he watched the woman he loved come through the revolving glass doors pulling luggage behind her.

She looked all bundled up in her leather coat, gloves, boots and a furry-looking hat that covered her head. It was cold outside, and according to the weather reports, it was the coldest it had been in New York all year. If the forecasters were right, the following days would get even more frigid with record-breaking temperatures. Combine that with snow and it was a recipe for disaster.

Jules opened the car door for her, and the wide-eyed look of surprise and the warm smile that lit her face caused a sensual jolt to his midsection. "Xavier! I didn't think I'd see you before I—"

He didn't give her a chance to finish what she was saying. In fact he barely gave her time to get settled in the backseat before he leaned over and captured her mouth with his. Damn, he needed her taste. He needed her. And at that moment there was no doubt in his mind that he loved her.

Their mouths mated hungrily and fused passionately as their tongues tangled in a wild and frenzied exchange that had him groaning. Thankfully, Jules drew the privacy shield closed without being told, and Xavier proceeded to pull Farrah into his lap. At that moment he couldn't fight the rush of desire that suddenly consumed him, making him hot, almost causing him to overload. She was returning his kiss measure for measure while sensation after glorious earth-shattering sensation tore into him.

They finally ended the kiss, but he kept his mouth close to hers, a breath away from her moist lips. The look in her eyes almost sent him over the edge. If he were to spread her out on the seat, strip her naked and take her, she wouldn't resist. There was no doubt in his mind that she wanted him as much as he wanted her.

But he wanted her to do more than just need him. He wanted her to love him as much as he loved her. To reach that goal he had to prove to her there was more between them than just the physical. That didn't mean he would stop making love to her. He just needed to find a balance between the physical and the emotional so that she would see she was not only desired but also loved.

"Now what were you about to say?" he asked, pulling her close to him while wrapping his arms around the back of the seat.

His gaze went immediately to her lips when they

began moving again. He liked kissing them, nibbling on them, licking them and doing all kinds of naughty things to them.

"I said I didn't think I would see you before I left," Farrah said.

Unable to resist any longer, Xavier leaned down and swiped a slow lick off her lips. "Did you honestly think I would let you leave without seeing you again and saying goodbye?"

"After last night I wasn't so sure."

Xavier pulled her closer to him. "Well, I am here, and in fact I intend to go back to Charlotte with you and Cam."

She blinked as if she wasn't certain she'd heard him correctly. "You're going back to Charlotte?"

"Yes, there's no reason for me to get stranded here, too. Besides, if the storm is as bad as the forecasters predict, the office will be closed anyway. I can fly back sometime next week to finalize things."

"Oh."

"I've got a favor to ask of you," he said, pulling off her gloves, needing to feel his skin enmeshed with hers.

"What?"

He entwined their fingers and felt the warmth of her flesh. He looked down at their joined hands in her lap. "I've been invited to several holiday parties and I want you to go as my date."

He felt her flinch but chose to ignore her reaction. "I had originally planned not to accept the invitations, but since we've decided to remove the limitations on our affair, I think it would be nice for us to share the holiday spirit, don't you?" Xavier figured those parties would be perfect for him and Farrah to be officially seen out together as a couple.

Farrah wasn't sure if what he was proposing would be nice or not. She certainly hadn't expected him to ask her out on a date so soon. And from what he'd said, it sounded as if it would be several dates. She knew it might sound pretty sleazy to some, but she much preferred sharing her time with him in the bedroom in a strictly physical and nonemotional affair. However, it had nothing to do with the reasons he had accused her of last night. To get him to believe that would be close to impossible.

Instead of answering his question, she posed one of her own. "How many parties are we talking about, Xavier?"

He leaned over and began nibbling on her neck, ears and the corners of her mouth. "Um, I think we're talking about three or four. And then there's the New Year's Eve party that Uriel and his wife, Ellie, are hosting at the lake."

She gazed up at him. "And you want me to attend all those parties with you?"

"Yes. Is there a reason why you can't? Have you made other plans for the holidays?"

Farrah inwardly sighed. Unfortunately, she hadn't made other plans. She figured on it being a low-key time for her. Her company was closed for ten days, and she had planned to buy a number of books and to stay in, relax and have a read-a-thon.

"Farrah?"

Why did he have to say her name in such a way that waylaid her senses and sent a ripple of desire through her? "Yes?"

"Have you made plans for the holidays already?"

"No, but—but—"

He lifted his head and stared down at her. "But what?"

How could she tell him that she wasn't comfortable dating the way normal couples did? How could she explain that she equated dating with establishing the foundation for something more serious, and she didn't do serious?

Instead of wasting her time explaining anything, she said, "Nothing. Going to all those events will be fine. Just let me know when and where and I'll meet you there."

Xavier threw his head back and laughed. "Sorry, sweetheart, but it doesn't quite work that way. I'll let you know when and where, but I'll pick you up. We won't show up in separate cars."

She nibbled on her bottom lip wondering why it mattered if they both ended up at the same place. But she didn't want to argue with him about it. She glanced out the window and noticed they had passed the exit for the airport. "Where are we going?"

"Back to my place to get luggage. When I talked

to you earlier I was at the office finishing up a few things."

She nodded. "And where's Mr. Cody?"

"Cameron has his own private car and will join us at the airport at the designated time."

"Okay."

She settled back against his chest, and when he shifted positions, she could feel his hard erection pressing against her backside. What she felt was a sure sign that he wanted her, so why wasn't he taking her?

As the car sped toward Long Island, she sat cuddled in Xavier's lap, thinking and wondering just what was going on in that mind of his.

Chapter 13

A few hours later Farrah entered her home, and Xavier walked in behind her. He thought the flight from New York had gone well, with Cam and Farrah chatting amiably during most of the trip. More than once Cam had shot him a look that had clearly asked, *Why have you kept her hidden?*

He closed the door, leaned against it and watched as she moved across the room and switched on a lamp. Although it was late afternoon, it had already been dark when the plane had landed. Two private cars had sat waiting on the airstrip. One had whisked Cameron home, and Xavier had placed Farrah and her luggage with him in the other.

Swallowing thickly, he recalled how tempted he had been to take her directly to his place instead of bringing her here. In the end, his common sense had won out. He had to be patient in his handling of her.

When she moved to turn on another lamp he glanced around thinking how he had missed coming here.

"Thanks for everything, Xavier, especially for making the arrangements to get me back home."

His gaze returned to her. "You're welcome."

Xavier straightened from leaning against the door, and his stomach clenched when she walked slowly toward him. He wasn't sure what she planned to do, but from the look in her eyes, he had a feeling he was in trouble.

When she reached him, she wrapped her arms around his neck. And when she tilted her face up to him, he lowered his head to give her what she wanted. What he wanted. The moment their lips connected, he slid his tongue in her mouth and began mating hungrily with hers. She melted into him, and he deepened the kiss by widening his mouth over hers.

He needed this contact as much as he needed to breathe. And she clung to him as if she felt the same way. For him, that was a good sign, one he intended to cultivate any way that he could. He reluctantly broke the kiss and whispered against her moist lips. "Come home with me tonight."

He saw the indecisiveness in her arched brow and knew why. One of their unspoken agreements had been he would visit her here. She'd preferred things that way because it had given her a semblance of control. What she didn't know, and what she would eventually discover, was that no matter how many roadblocks she erected, he intended to rush right through each and every one of them.

When she didn't say anything, he leaned down to place kisses around her mouth. "I figure we could grab something to eat at the Racetrack Café and go to my place to watch a movie and then go to sleep."

"Sleep?" she asked in a deep, raspy tone.

"Yes, if that's what you want to do," he said in a husky voice. "But would you really want to?"

Farrah threw her head back and groaned deep in her throat when the tip of Xavier's tongue became naughty and began licking all around her mouth. The man was torturing her something awful. She tried pushing the thoughts from her mind that he was asking her to relinquish control by doing something atypical in their relationship.

However, she *had* agreed to an unlimited affair with him, hadn't she? And she did want to make love to him again, didn't she? Should it matter if it was his bed or hers? His home or hers?

"Farrah?"

She met his gaze. The look she saw in his eyes was enough to make her panties wet. "No, I don't want to sleep," she heard herself saying. "And yes, I want to spend the night at your place."

Farrah moved around her bedroom unpacking her things, while at the same time tossing a few items into an overnight bag. The private car had taken Xavier home where he would get his car and come back for her in an hour.

Snapping her overnight bag shut, she moved from her bedroom toward the living room, intent on making sure she was ready when he returned. Tremors of anticipation were racing through her at the thought that he would be taking her back to the place where they had met. A place where a number of his friends, as well as hers, hung out.

She nearly jumped when the doorbell sounded, and moved toward the door. She looked through the peep-hole, and sensations flooded her insides. It was Xavier, and as she had done, he had taken time to change clothes. Opening the door, she saw he was no longer wearing a suit but had changed into a pair of jeans and a shirt. And this was the first time he had appeared on her doorstep without his signature bottle of wine.

She felt his gaze roam over her, and when he smiled, she couldn't help but smile, too. "Ready?" he asked, taking her overnight bag from her hand.

"Yes."

He stepped back, and after she locked the door behind her, he took her hand and escorted her to his two-seater sports car.

"Did you enjoy your meal?" Xavier asked Farrah a short while later at the Racetrack Café.

The popular bar and grill in town was jointly owned by several drivers on the NASCAR circuit. Over the years it had become one of his favorite places to eat and to hang out, especially on the weekends

Tonight the place was crowded, understandably so since there was a live band every Friday night. Couples were on the dance floor, and he couldn't wait to get out there himself. The need to hold Farrah in his arms was hitting him hard.

"Yes, everything was wonderful."

"Do you remember that we met here?" He wondered if she remembered that night like he did.

She smiled. "Yes, I know. It was girls night out for me and Natalie. She had her eyes on Donovan and my eyes were on you. I thought you were hot."

Xavier chuckled. One of the things he liked about Farrah was her honesty. She was up front with her responses. "You thought so?"

"Yes, I still do," she said softly at the same time one of her bare feet intentionally rubbed against his pants leg.

He held her gaze, fully aware of what she was trying to do. It wouldn't take much to push him over the edge. She was ready for them to leave and go to his place to be alone.

"Hey, you two, when did you get back?"

He glanced up to find Donovan Steele and his wife, Natalie, standing at their table. Immediately Farrah was out of her seat to give her best friend a hug, while likewise, he stood to shake Donovan's hand and invite him and Natalie to join them.

"We decided to head back before the snowstorm hit,"

he said, smiling over at Donovan. "Cameron made that possible since he was anxious to return to Charlotte anyway. We caught a ride back on his private plane."

Donovan chuckled. "I can just imagine Cam wanting to get back. Now that Vanessa is pregnant, he doesn't like being away from her for too long."

"So you didn't get any shopping in?" Natalie asked Farrah, grinning.

"Are you kidding?" Farrah laughed. "You know I don't do cold weather well. I was ready to come home the minute the temperatures dropped below twenty."

Xavier leaned back in his chair and noticed Farrah seemed comfortable with them being seen together as a couple tonight. During the course of their meal, several people they knew had stopped by their table to say hello.

"Since the two of you have finished eating, will you be leaving here soon?" Donovan asked.

Xavier glanced over at Farrah and saw the hopeful look in her eyes but chose to ignore it. "Not until we get a few dances in, starting now, so please excuse us," he said, standing up and extending his hand out to Farrah when he heard the band play a slow number. She took it and stood.

He was grateful she wasn't upset that he was stalling about leaving. But he wanted her to enjoy doing things with him other than making love. He pulled her into his arms the moment their feet touched the dance floor. Wrapping his arms around her waist, he drank in her luscious fragrance. "Do you remember the first time we danced here together?" he asked, angling his head and leaning his mouth close to her ear.

She nodded, tilting her head back to look up at him. "Yes, it was right after we spent an hour or so in the game room. You beat me at everything that night. Pool. Darts. Pinball."

He chuckled. "Yes, but you weren't so bad. In fact I thought you were pretty good."

She seemed pleased with his compliment. "Really?"

"Yes, really. I think we need to play a few of those games again sometime."

She studied his gaze. "But not tonight."

He chuckled. "No, definitely not tonight."

He pulled her tighter in his arms, and she rested her head against his chest. He felt his desire for her growing and his love right along with it. He tightened his arm around her even more, and glancing over at their table, he saw Donovan and Natalie watching them with curious eyes. But he didn't care. The only thing he cared about was the feel of her in his arms. The woman whose head was pressed against his heart. A heart that belonged to her whether she knew it or not.

They moved to the slow music, and luckily for him, when the song ended, another slow one began. And just like before, he held her close. At one point he rested his lips close to her ear and sang parts of the song to her. In between the lyrics, he whispered just what he wanted to do to her later. And he was as detailed and explicit as he could be.

When the song came to an end, before they parted, Farrah leaned closed to him and whispered, "Don't be all talk. Do it."

Xavier decided to accept her challenge. He took her hand in his and led her back over to their table. After quickly gathering their coats and her purse, they bid good-night to their friends and left.

They didn't share much conversation in the car. Instead, Farrah stared out the window at the moonless sky, although there were a number of bright stars overhead.

She figured there was nothing left to be said between them since they both knew what they wanted. But that didn't keep her from anticipating what was in store. She didn't have any regrets about them being together and couldn't help thinking how easy it had been to be out with him tonight. She had enjoyed herself before dinner, during dinner and after dinner.

They had discussed a number of topics, and when people who knew them had approached their table, it hadn't bothered her when she could tell they assumed she and Xavier were an item. Even when Donovan and Natalie had shown up and joined them, she hadn't been bothered by the knowing looks Natalie had given her.

Farrah's attention was pulled back to the present when they came to the entrance of Xavier's subdivision, and he pulled up to the security gate. Moments later he drove through. Most of the homes they passed were adorned with holiday decorations. It then dawned on her that she hadn't bothered putting up a tree since her divorce from Dustin. At one time she used to fully embrace the merriment of the season and would look forward to all the holiday festivities.

When Xavier's car pulled into the driveway to his home and the garage door went up, she felt an anxiousness in the pit of her stomach. She was here at the place he considered his primary home. After the garage door closed behind him and he'd brought the car to a stop, he killed the engine before glancing over at her and smiling. "Welcome to my home, Farrah."

There was something about what he said that sent a warm feeling through her. "Thanks for bringing me here."

And she truly meant it. There *was* something about being here, being a part of Xavier's element and sharing his personal space that had her feeling emotions she had never felt before.

He opened the car door and she watched as he moved around the front of the vehicle to open the door for her. He extended his hand to her, and she took it, and then, surprising her, he whisked her off her feet and into his arms.

"Xavier!"

He lowered his head and captured the squeal from her lips, effectively silencing her while mating his mouth hungrily and greedily with hers. His tongue was devouring her, escalating her desire and longing for him as he took her mouth with a mastery that made her groan.

Moments later he released her mouth and began walking with her toward his back door. Desire began spiraling through her when he opened the door. She didn't say a word. She just stared up at him while he continued to hold her in his arms.

He pushed the door open and carried her over the threshold. She could barely see her surroundings as he swiftly moved through his kitchen, dining room and living room and then carried her up the stairs.

Xavier walked down a hall before finally entering a dark bedroom. He placed her in the middle of the bed before turning on a lamp to bring light into the room. It was then that she looked at him and saw the heat within his gaze. Her eyes roamed all over every square inch of his muscular body after he removed his coat and tossed it aside. The muscles bulging beneath his shirt made her appreciate the fact he was a man with the ability to make her mind incapable of thought. With Xavier all she could do was feel.

He unbuttoned his shirt, then removed it to reveal one incredibly hot-looking chest dusted with hair she wouldn't mind running her fingers through or burying her nose in, while inhaling his masculine scent.

When her gaze moved from his chest to meet his eyes, he said, "In case you're wondering what I'm doing, I'm about to prove to you, Farrah Langley, that I am not all talk."

Chapter 14

No, he wasn't all talk, Farrah thought a short while later as his engorged erection pushed through her womanly folds to join their bodies as one.

Already she had climaxed from his mouth twice, and every single inch of her was still humming for more. How was he able to do that? He used his mouth in ways that should be outlawed.

Once he had stripped every stitch of clothing from her body and encased his huge erection into a condom, he had joined her in bed. A slow, sensual smile had touched his lips when he pulled her into his arms, and anticipation had rammed through her, making her want him that much more.

"At last," she whispered when she felt the strength of him continue to push through her. He lifted her hips in his big hands, holding her steady while he pushed inside of her to the hilt. And then he threw his head back and growled satisfaction. He began moving inside of her, sending sensations from where their bodies were joined to every part of her body, touching every single nerve ending and making breath whoosh from her lungs.

Each stroke, each tantalizing thrust, made her moan his name over and over. He lowered his head to her breasts and captured a nipple between his lips and began sucking on it like it was the best thing he'd ever tasted. She felt on the verge of total sensuous madness and ultimate fulfillment.

"Farrah!"

She knew the moment his body exploded, and she tightened her legs around his waist when she felt him driven to yet another orgasm. She screamed his name when she felt herself losing control, digging her fingers deep in his shoulders while doing so. He continued to thrust into her, over and over again.

It was only then he slumped off her, still keeping her in his arms and their bodies connected. Even now it seemed he wasn't ready to let her go. And for the moment, as he held her in his arms, there was no other place she'd rather be.

The sound of cabinet doors opening and closing downstairs made Xavier open his eyes to squint against the sunlight coming in through his window. He smiled, realizing he was in his bedroom. His bed. And he had made love to Farrah in it last night. To him that was a major accomplishment.

He gazed up at the ceiling remembering last night. Oh, what a night. After removing his own clothes he had proceeded to remove hers before tasting every single inch of her body. Her full sweet breasts had been heavenly, the dark nipples meant for sucking and licking.

The sounds she'd made when his mouth touched her body only made him want to do even more things to her. And they were things that had made his erection swell even more.

By the time he had eased between her legs, while she had clutched his shoulders tight and wrapped her long legs around his waist, he'd known they would be having orgasms all over the place. They had. The mere memory had his erection throbbing. He wanted her again, and he wanted her now.

Easing out of bed, he slipped into the jeans he had discarded last night. He went into the bathroom to quickly wash his face and brush his teeth and couldn't help but smile when he saw her toothbrush already in the holder beside his.

He moved slowly down the stairs, and when his nose picked up the aroma of coffee, he increased his pace. He rounded the corner to the kitchen and stopped dead in his tracks. Farrah was standing at the refrigerator, leaning over to look inside and wearing the shirt he'd worn last night. It barely covered her rear end and he could clearly see the luscious swell of her butt cheeks, which meant she wasn't wearing any panties.

It could have been his groan that made her aware he was behind her. She turned, and they stared at each other, not saying anything. It was as if time stood still.

He finally moved, crossed the room to her and, without saying a word, he lifted her into his arms, carried her over to the table and sat down in the chair with her straddling his lap. He wanted her. Now.

He took her mouth, mated with it voraciously while she took matters into her own hands by lowering his zipper to release his erection from bondage. Once free, his erection swelled in anticipation, and when he released her mouth, he whispered against her moist lips, "I want to come inside of you."

He knew just what he was saying, exactly what he was asking. They both were fully aware that since the night they'd met neither had indulged in sex with anyone else. And as far as he was concerned, they wouldn't be making love with anyone but each other from now on. They both had good health records, so as far as he was concerned, there was no reason they couldn't be skin-to-skin, flesh-to-flesh and make love with the purpose of giving each other the most primitive pleasure possible. He'd never released his semen inside a woman before but wanted to do so with her. He just hoped and prayed that she went along with it.

He watched her nervously nibble on her bottom lip, which meant she was considering his request. "Why?" she asked.

"Because every time I sank my body into yours," he whispered, "I wanted to know what it's like to feel you without any barriers and to know when I come I will fill you with the very essence of me. Not for the purpose of making a baby, but for the purpose of knowing how it feels to mingle my semen with your juices when we share pleasure."

His pulse throbbed painfully in his throat as he waited for her to make the next move. Her grip on his erection tightened, and she lifted her body off his lap so he could slide inside of her. As he began pushing forward, she groaned while her muscles clenched him all the way. And when he met her gaze he saw a mirror of desire so heated it almost took his breath away.

He pushed farther inside of her and knew the exact moment the physical and the emotional became one, merging in a way that robbed him of any coherent thought other than to be with her like this. And when he began moving, he felt her heated flesh consume him with every thrust. Unable to retain hold of his sanity, he leaned over and devoured her mouth as he gave her body and the chair one hell of a workout.

And then it happened. An explosion that nearly knocked the chair from under them. In a mad rush his semen filled her, triggering her climax. She screamed his name, and he gritted his teeth as he continued to pump into her. Hard. Fast. He was giving her all he had with no holding back. This was the way it was supposed to be, he thought. This was the way he wanted it. And

from her deep, guttural scream this was the way she
wanted it as well.

Little did she know that for them this was only the
beginning.

Farrah sat at Xavier's kitchen table and glanced
out the window that faced the majestic Palisades Golf
Course. Already golfers were moving about. Luckily the
curtains had been drawn when they'd made out in the
very chair she was sitting in a short while ago. Xavier
had assured her that even if the curtain had been open it
would have been highly unlikely that anyone would have
seen what they'd done in his kitchen. Still, the thought
couldn't help but make her blush.

She took another sip of her coffee as she moved her
gaze from the window to the man standing at the stove
preparing pancakes. He hadn't bothered to snap up his
jeans that hung low on lean hips, and they looked so
darn good on his hard masculine thighs and fine-as-
a-dime backside. Her gaze traveled upward and did a
wide sweep of his hairy chest, tight abs, well-defined
arm muscles and wide shoulders.

She moved her gaze upward, past his broad shoulders
to his face. He had long lashes, the kind most women
would kill for. And the shadow darkening his jaw indi-
cated he hadn't bothered to shave. Then there were his
lips, full and inviting. She felt heat flood her stomach
when she remembered all the things those lips and his
mouth had done to her.

She released a deep breath, suddenly feeling the

effect of the caffeine. The effect of Xavier Kane. The man had a gorgeous body, and he most certainly knew how to use it.

"You like what you see, Farrah?"

She blinked, wondering how he'd known she was staring at him when he was supposed to be concentrating on fixing breakfast. He looked up and smiled before turning around to face her while leaning his hip against the kitchen counter.

"How could I not like what I see? You're a straight guy, pretty well-off and you look pretty darn good in a pair of jeans. And you can make me purr in the bedroom. According to some women, a man with those qualities is a rarity these days."

He lifted a brow. "Some women?"

"Yes, those looking for a mate."

"Oh, I see." He didn't say anything for a minute and then asked, "What are you doing next Saturday night?"

She blinked. His question had caught her off guard. She hesitated for a second and then said, "I don't recall having any plans. Why?"

"I'd like you to go to a party with me."

She placed her coffee cup down, feeling anxiety set in. "A party?"

"Yes."

Her anxiety increased. Although he had mentioned attending parties with him, she wasn't prepared to do so this soon.

"It's being given by Donovan's brother Morgan and

his wife, Lena. A holiday fundraiser to benefit under-privileged kids."

Instead of saying anything, Farrah picked up her cup to take a sip of her coffee. She needed to think about that. She didn't know Morgan Steele that well, but she had known Lena for years. As a real estate agent, Lena had been the one to sell her and Dustin their first home, and four years later she had sought out Lena's services to find her another place after their divorce.

"Farrah?"

She glanced up and met Xavier's gaze. His expression didn't give anything away, but she had a feeling he fully expected her to turn him down, although she *had* agreed to the affair without limitations. In a way, she felt foolish for letting past pain dictate how she lived her life.

She forced her eyes away from his to glance out the window, knowing she couldn't hide behind her pain forever. Maybe it was time to take a stand and finally move on. Something she hadn't done and something it seemed Xavier was hell-bent on forcing her to do.

She glanced back at him and swallowed deeply before saying, "Yes. I'll go to the party with you."

Chapter 15

Farrah stared at herself in the full-length mirror. When was the last time she had dressed to please a man? And as much as she'd tried convincing herself she'd purchased this dress because she'd liked it, deep down she'd bought it because she figured Xavier would like it. It was blue, his favorite color, and the style of the dress showed off her figure. Even Natalie had said so when the two had gone shopping.

At least there would be people at the party she would know besides the host and hostess. Donovan and Natalie would be there, as well as other members of the Steele family. And Xavier had mentioned a couple of his godbrothers would be in attendance as well.

Last weekend, she had ended up spending the entire time at Xavier's home. On Saturday night he had brought her back home to get more clothes and to dress for a movie.

She laughed softly to herself when she thought how Xavier had threatened never to take her to a movie again if she had to cry through the entire feature. She hadn't been able to help it, convinced during most of the film the hero was going to lose his life and never return to the heroine.

When she heard the doorbell sound, she slowly inhaled a breath of air and gave herself time to release it. Xavier had returned to New York on Tuesday to finalize a few things and had called every night to see how she was doing. He'd returned to Charlotte late last night and had called her this morning to invite her to his place for breakfast. Unfortunately, she had been on her way out the door for her hair and nail appointment.

As she headed for the door, a part of her wondered what on earth she was doing by letting another man get under her skin. But in reality, he'd done more than get under her skin. He had licked every part of it at one time or another. She would be the first to admit that although she was still trying with all her might to keep her guard in place, the time she was beginning to spend with him outside of the bedroom was awakening something within her that she thought had long ago died a brutal death. She could actually say she enjoyed spending time with a man in something other than a sexual affair.

She stopped walking and squeezed her eyes shut for a second, remembering why she had broken things off between them six months ago. Why wasn't the thought of becoming too close not scaring her out of her wits now?

A shiver ran down her spine as she opened her eyes and resumed walking. It was hard to describe what she was feeling these days. It was as if each and every time Xavier touched her he was branding her for life. She knew the idea of such a thing sounded absolutely crazy and probably was, but she couldn't let go of the question running through her head. Why was she comfortable with how things were between them now?

She opened the door, and he stood there, leaning in her doorway, and as usual, looking as sexy as ever. For some reason, he seemed even more so today, dressed in a pair of jeans, a white shirt and a chocolate brown suede jacket. He smiled at her in a way that deepened the lines around his lips and brought out a dimple she rarely saw. And then she saw something flame to life in his gaze, and her heart began pounding in her chest. She felt sensual stirrings in the pit of her stomach.

"Xavier," she said in a raspy voice that she couldn't hide. "Welcome back to Charlotte." She took a step back to let him inside.

"It's good to be back. I missed you." And then he reached out for her, pulled her into his arms and captured her mouth in his. A part of her understood his craving since it mirrored her own hunger. He said he'd missed her. She honestly didn't know what to make of that. They had been together nearly a year before and had gone weeks without seeing each other, and not once had he ever admitted to missing her.

But tonight he had.

He finally pulled his mouth away but rested his forehead against hers, drawing in a deep breath while she did likewise. He then whispered against her moist lips, "It wouldn't take much to strip you naked right now."

"What's stopping you?" she murmured, taking a quick lick of his lips and causing his erection to jump. She felt it and couldn't help but smile at his body's response to her words.

His gaze roamed over her before returning to her eyes. "It's tempting, sweetheart, but we have a party to attend."

She leaned forward and wrapped her arms around his neck. "You mean you'd rather go to a party tonight than stay here and spend some productive time with me?"

A smile spread across his lips. "No, but I plan for us to go to that damn party and when it's over I'll bring you back here and get a lot of productive time in."

"You might be too tired."

He threw his head back and laughed. "Not on your life, sweetheart, so come on and let's go. The sooner we can make an appearance at the party, the sooner we can get back here and get naughty."

She couldn't help but smile. "I'm holding you to that, Xavier Kane."

* * *

"Will you be withdrawing your membership from the club, X?"

Xavier glanced up at one of his godbrothers, Virgil Bougard. "What gives you that idea, V?" he asked, taking a sip of his wine.

"The way you're acting with Farrah Langley. Tonight's the first time I've seen you out with a woman in a long time and unless I'm seeing wrong, you're quite taken with her."

Xavier smiled. No, Virgil wasn't seeing wrong. But then, even if he were to explain how things were, Virgil wouldn't understand.

"And what do you think you see, V?" he couldn't help but ask. He could tell Virgil was getting annoyed with his evasiveness.

Virgil frowned. "I see you acting almost as bad as Uriel. At least he's married. Just look at you now. You're talking to me but not once have you taken your eyes off Farrah."

Xavier knew that much was true. He had pretty much hung by Farrah's side most of the evening. Only when Natalie and Vanessa had come and grabbed her had he sought out Virgil's company for a while.

"Xavier?"

He glanced back to Virgil. "Yes?"

"I said that—"

"Mind if I join you guys?"

He glanced over at the woman who walked up. Marti Goshay. They'd been involved in a sex-only affair a few years ago that hadn't even lasted a month. That was all of her he could take, especially when she'd begun hinting at a serious affair that she'd wanted to end in marriage.

"Would it matter if we said that we did mind?" Virgil asked the woman.

Xavier had to keep from smiling. He'd forgotten there was bad blood between Virgil and Marti. Some claimed she was the reason her sister had dumped Virgil a few years ago over some lie Marti had told.

Ignoring Virgil, Marti turned her attention to Xavier. "I thought I'd give you my business card. I hadn't heard from you in a while and figured you probably didn't know my phone number had changed."

He nodded as he accepted the card she handed him. Not that he would use it. He intended to toss it in the trash at the next opportunity. Of course, Marti would think the only reason he hadn't contacted her in almost two years was because he didn't have her new phone number. The woman really thought a lot of herself. She was attractive, true enough, but her beauty was only on the outside. Farrah's beauty, he thought, was both inside and out.

"How would you like to attend the Tina Turner concert with me next weekend, Xavier?" she asked him.

"I'll be busy next weekend."

Virgil decided not to be so subtle. "He's involved with someone, Marti. Move on."

The woman seemed amused by that bit of news.

"Who? Definitely not the woman you brought here tonight," she said smiling. "Everybody knows Farrah Langley couldn't hold on to her husband. He was involved in an affair, so what does that tell you?"

Xavier turned his dark, laser sharp eyes on Marti and said, "It tells me the man was a damn fool." He walked off, leaving Virgil to deal with her, knowing without a doubt that his godbrother could.

"I thought the party was nice, Xavier. Thanks for bringing me."

He glanced over at Farrah as they pulled out of Morgan's driveway. "Thank you for coming."

Farrah leaned back against the headrest and closed her eyes. The party had been nice, and she hadn't once felt awkward being seen out with him. In fact, she'd read a lot of envy in the gazes of a number of women. What she'd told Xavier earlier tonight was true. He would be a great catch for any woman.

Even her.

She snapped her eyes back open and glanced over at him. His full attention seemed to be on driving, but her full attention was on him. What made her put herself in the group with all those other women when she wasn't interested in a serious relationship? She didn't think of Xavier in terms of a good catch, but rather a perfect lover. What if she began seeing him in a whole new light?

She shook her head and then turned her attention to the objects outside the car window, refusing to go there. The only reason she was thinking such things was because of how good she felt. She had enjoyed a good party and now she was looking forward to an even better night. That had to be it. It couldn't be any other reason.

"What are you doing next weekend, Farrah?"

She glanced back over at Xavier. "Why do you want to know?"

"I have tickets to the *Nutcracker* and was wondering if you'd go with me?"

She drew in a deep breath. Now was the time to tell him that although she had enjoyed herself with him tonight, they shouldn't overdo it. But for some reason, she couldn't fix her mouth to say that. Especially when she enjoyed the *Nutcracker*.

"Yes, I'd love to go with you," she heard herself saying.

He smiled. "Good."

Farrah looked back out of the car's window, not sure if it was good or not.

Chapter 16

Farrah tried shifting to another position and discovered she couldn't, due to the masculine body still connected to hers. Ever since Xavier had stopped using a condom, he liked drifting off to sleep with his manhood still inside of her and one of his legs thrown over hers. More than once over the past few weeks, she had awakened from the feel of his erection stretching her inner muscles as it enlarged inside of her.

It was hard to believe that next week would be Christmas, and so far she had been Xavier's date to four parties and to the *Nutcracker*. Since they ran into most of the same people at all the events, she knew everyone thought they were having a hot and heavy love affair... and she would have to agree with them.

That thought no longer bothered her, and each and

every day she was beginning to feel more and more comfortable with him and how their relationship was going. Just last week he'd flown her to New York to spend a few days with him while he'd wrapped up business there. She had stayed with him at his home, spending her days shopping and her nights in his bed.

Needing to go to the bathroom, she tapped him on the shoulder and his sleep-laden sexy eyes stared into hers. "I have to go to the bathroom," she whispered.

He lifted his leg off hers and disconnected their bodies before flipping on his stomach. From the sound of his even breathing, he had gone back to sleep within seconds. She smiled as she eased out of the bed. Poor baby, she thought. Evidently she had worn him out.

The light shining from the bathroom showed their clothes were scattered all over the floor. They had begun stripping the moment they had entered her bedroom. How they'd made it up the stairs with their clothes on was beyond her.

After using the bathroom, she was returning to the bed and decided to gather up the scattered clothing along the way and toss them on a chair. She picked a business card off the floor that evidently had fallen out of Xavier's jacket. She was about to put it back inside the pocket when she read the words someone had scrawled on the back.

Call me. You won't regret it.

She frowned when she flipped the card over. Marti Goshay, Attorney-at-Law.

Her frown deepened. Although she didn't know Marti

Goshay personally, she knew of her. And she'd known from that night at the party that Morgan and Lena had guessed the woman had the hots for Xavier. Farrah had heard from Natalie that Xavier and Marti had dated a while back, and from the looks Marti had had in her eyes whenever she'd glanced at Xavier, the woman wanted him back.

Farrah had been talking to Natalie and Vanessa that particular night and had seen Marti hand Xavier her business card. He had taken it, and at the time Farrah had wondered why. Now she wanted to know why he'd kept it. That had been almost two weeks ago. Hadn't he claimed he wanted a long-term affair with her because he was tired of women coming on to him? So why hadn't he let Marti Goshay know he was already involved?

Not even bothering to fight back the anger and jealousy she suddenly felt, she quickly moved to the bed to tap Xavier on the shoulder. "Wake up, Xavier. You need to leave. Now."

She had to tap him a couple more times before he finally awoke. "Xavier, you need to leave."

He lifted his head and flipped on his back to stare up at her with sleep-filled eyes. "What's wrong?"

"Nothing other than this," she said, dropping the business card onto his naked chest.

He rubbed a hand down his face before picking up the card. He considered it for a moment and then tossed it on her nightstand. "Come back to bed, Farrah."

His command angered her even more. "I won't, and

I want you out of my bed. Now," she said, looming over him, in his face.

Instead of moving, he stretched out, placed his hands behind his head and stared up at her. "Why?"

She rolled angry eyes. "I just told you why."

"No, you didn't."

And before she could blink, he had reached out and grabbed her hands and tumbled her down in the bed with him. He shifted his position, and now she was the one on her back with him looming over her. "Now tell me why you're upset, Farrah."

"That business card fell out of your jacket."

He shrugged. "And?"

That one word seemed to make her angrier. "And that was enough."

He chuckled. "I care to differ. Marti Goshay gave me that business card at Morgan and Lena's party."

"But you kept it."

"Only because I'd forgotten about it. I had intended to throw it away." Now it was his eyes that darkened with anger. "And just what are you accusing me of?"

"What do you think?"

For a few seconds Xavier just stared down at her, and then a smile replaced his anger. "You're jealous."

That observation really riled her. "I am *not* jealous. I detest men who can't be trusted. Now get off of me."

Xavier released her and eased off the bed. He moved across the room and slumped down in the chair. "So you're saying I can't be trusted because you found a business card in my jacket?"

She sat up in bed. "A business card from an old girlfriend who said to call her."

"And you figured I would?"

"You kept the card, Xavier."

She fought back the tears. She wouldn't tell him that was the first sign she'd gotten that Dustin was cheating. It was the first one she'd gotten and the main one she'd overlooked, thinking there was nothing to it. She had been a fool not to catch the early warning signs. She wouldn't be a fool ever again.

"Does your mistrust of me have anything to do with that ass you were married to?"

"And if it does?"

He held her gaze. "Then I want you to stop."

"Stop?"

"Yes. Stop comparing me to him, Farrah." He slowly shook his head. "You still don't get it, do you?"

She crossed her arms over her chest. "And just what am I supposed to be getting?"

"The fact that no other woman interests me because I love you."

Her mouth dropped open. "Love me? That's crazy."

He eased to his feet. "Maybe. And what's even crazier is that I believe you love me back. You're just afraid to admit it. However, your overblown jealousy just proved I'm right."

She glared over at him. "You're not right. I don't love you."

He smiled. "Yes, you do and please don't say what we've been sharing was nothing but sex. Sex between us is good—hell, it's unbelievable, Farrah. But nothing can be that good unless there's some heavy-duty love thrown into the mix. For the past three weeks I've deliberately and painstakingly tried proving to you that we're good together, in or out of bed. Think about it." He then moved to walk away.

She floundered for a response and then asked, "And just where do you think you're going?"

"To take a shower," he called over his shoulder as he kept walking. He went into the bathroom and closed the door behind him.

A frustrated Farrah reclined on her back and stared up at the ceiling when she heard the shower going. How dare he insinuate that she loved him just because she'd gotten tiffed over finding that business card. Any woman would be upset. Wouldn't she?

She turned her head toward his pillow and breathed in deeply to inhale the scent he'd left behind. And then she closed her eyes, and memories began flooding her brain. The magic of everything she and Xavier had shared touched her deeply. Did he really mean it when he said that he loved her?

She considered the possibility for a second and knew it was true. What other man would have taken the time to deliberately take their affair out of the bedroom? And each and every time she'd gone out on a date with him, she had enjoyed it immensely. He'd been adept at balancing the physical part of their relationship with the emotional.

And she knew, believed in her heart, that he was

nothing like Dustin. Xavier could be trusted. He would never deliberately hurt her, use her or abuse what they had together. He would only love her.

Tears sprang into her eyes, and she wiped them away as she eased off the bed and headed toward the bathroom. He was so right. He wasn't Dustin, and her ex couldn't compare to Xavier in any way.

He was right about something else, too. She did love him, and it was about time she showed him how much.

A spray of water poured over Xavier's body as he stood underneath the showerhead. A part of him always regretted washing away Farrah's scent; he much preferred to wear it all day.

He hoped he'd given her something to think about, although that was not how he'd wanted to blurt out that he loved her. He'd pretty much envisioned a romantic candlelit dinner on Christmas night where he would pour his heart and soul out to her before asking her to marry him. But at least now she knew how he felt, and the way she'd gotten in a tiff about Marti's business card had sent hopeful chills up his spine.

If she thought for one minute he was going to let her end things between them again, she had another thought coming. He was in for the long haul, and the sooner she admitted to herself that she loved him, the better it would be for the both of them. Then they could get on with their lives. Together.

He reached up to turn off the water when the shower

door opened and she stood there. Naked. Beautiful. He leaned against the tile wall. His heart began doing jumping jacks in his chest when she stepped into the shower stall with him. "I didn't know you planned to take a shower with me," he said throatily, feeling every word torn deep in his lungs.

Instead of saying anything, she grabbed the soap and lathered her hands and then reached for his chest. He grabbed her hands to stop her. Whenever they showered together, she always lathered him all over. She was acting as if nothing had changed between them. But things had, and it was time for her to acknowledge that fact.

He held her hands tightly in his and met her gaze. "Tell me, Farrah. Don't show me anymore. Whether you wanted to or not, you've been showing me each and every time we made love. Now I want you to tell me."

She shook her head. "I can't."

He rubbed a finger gently across her cheek. "Yes, you can, baby. You're not the only one who's ever been hurt by love."

Her mouth pressed into a thin line, and for a minute he thought that maybe he had pushed her too far, had asked too much of her. But then she took a step toward him and reached up to wrap her arms around his neck while water sprayed down on them both. He reached behind him and turned off the water and turned back to her. "Tell me."

She inhaled deeply and met his gaze. "I love you, Xavier," she then said softly. "I've loved you for a long time. I've been too scared to admit it to myself. I tried denying it by sending you away. And then when I ran into you in New York, I convinced myself that a holiday fling was all I wanted. But I know now that would not have been the case. I will always love you and I want you."

He lowered his mouth to hers at the same time his hands spread across her backside to bring her closer to him. He fully understood what she'd been going through. It had taken him a while to recover from Dionne, so he knew why she'd been hesitant to give her love freely again. But each and every day he would show her, tell her, prove to her just how much she was loved, wanted and cherished.

He continued to take her mouth in agonizing pleasure, tasting her as their tongues tangled, mated in a dance of possession and non-restraint. He wasn't the only one coming unleashed. She was deliberately tempting him by rubbing her body against his, cradling his manhood between her open thighs. She moaned into his mouth, and the sound sent sensuous shivers all the way up his spine.

Xavier broke off the kiss and drew in a deep breath. He studied the face staring up at him, and it was all he could do to maintain his control and not sweep her into his arms and take her back to bed.

"I was determined to prove to you it wasn't just about sex with us, Farrah," he said, reaching out to brush back wet hair from her face.

"And you did." A smile touched her lips. "But the sex was still good."

He chuckled. "It will always be good between us. I love you."

"And I love you, too."

Xavier lowered his head, capturing her mouth again. He knew at that moment that their life together was just beginning.

Epilogue

Six months later

"I now pronounce you man and wife. You may kiss your bride, Xavier."

Xavier pulled Farrah into his arms and kissed her deeply. Moments later when he felt one of his godbrothers poke him in the side, he winced before releasing her mouth. He'd gotten carried away, but that was okay. It was his wedding day, and he intended to let everyone know just what a happy man he was.

A short while later at the wedding reception, he stood on the sidelines watching Farrah toss her bouquet to all the single ladies when one of the men standing by his side said, "You're officially out of the club now, X."

He glanced over to his godbrothers, the ones who

were still bachelors in demand—Virgil, Winston, York and Zion. "I know, but I have no regrets."

He glanced back to Farrah. In her wedding gown, she looked simply beautiful. She met his gaze and smiled. He hoped one day each of his godbrothers would have a reason to lose membership in the club as well. He was convinced that nothing could replace a good woman in a man's life. Nothing.

"It's time for our dance," Farrah said, walking straight into his outstretched arms.

Her small hands felt secure in his as he led her to the dance floor. He couldn't wait until later tonight when he had her alone. In the morning, they would leave for a two-week honeymoon in Hawaii.

Xavier caught the eye of his friend Galen Steele, who was also one of Donovan's cousins from Phoenix. Galen, who'd been a devout bachelor, had gotten married himself a few months ago. From the smile he still wore on his face, Galen, like Xavier, had no regrets about moving from a being single man to a truly happily married one.

Farrah smiled up at him when they reached the dance floor. "Are you happy, sweetheart?" he asked her.

"Yes, I am truly happy. What about you?"

Instead of answering he leaned down and kissed her. After hearing a number of catcalls and whistles he figured he would let her mouth go.

"Did that answer your question?" he asked, whispering against her moist lips.

She laughed softly as she looked up at him. "Oh, yes, that pretty much summed it up."

Xavier pulled her tighter into his arms, feeling all of the love in his heart. He would have to agree. That pretty much summed it up.

* * * * *

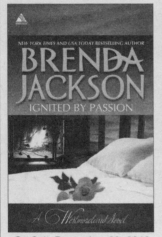
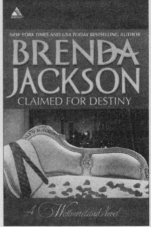

REQUEST YOUR FREE BOOKS!

2 FREE NOVELS
PLUS 2 FREE GIFTS!

KIMANI
ROMANCE
TM

Love's ultimate destination!

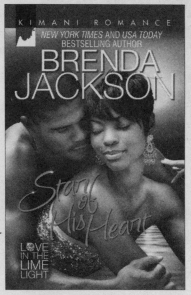

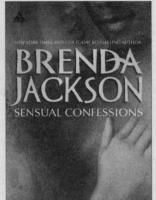